VERONICA CHASE

MYSTERIES

The Malibu Beach Mystery

VERONICA CHASE

MYSTERIES

 1

The Malibu Beach Mystery

First IUniverse trade paperback edition ©2003

VERONICA CHASE

MYSTERIES

Collect the entire series!

1. Malibu Beach Mystery
2. Clue of the Shattered Heart
3. Secret of Winstead Manor

1

A New Beginning

"Look Ronnie, there's the sign," Bryan exclaimed. "We're finally here! Hollywood, California, we've arrived!"

Veronica Chase glanced in the direction her brother was pointing. The famous white letters of the "Hollywood" sign were leaping from the mountain, welcoming them to the *"City of Angels."* Suddenly, it seemed real. She always wanted to live in California. Washington was a beautiful state, but grew tired of constant cloudy days and rain which could drag on for months. Now she was in sunny California, and couldn't deny how gorgeous the weather was. The sky was the most beautiful blue, there wasn't a cloud in sight.

A loud honk from an *SUV* in the next lane shattered Veronica's thoughts.

"Veronica, keep your eyes on the road! Do you want to get in an accident?" her brother questioned in a teasing tone. "Don't forget you are carrying precious cargo in this car, ME!"

Veronica had shoulder length dark, and beautiful blue eyes. Her dark complexion and shiny black hair gave her an exotic look. Her mother told her she had a look perfect for modeling, but she always told her mother the same thing, she wanted a career which would somehow help others. It had been difficult living in a household with two working parents. Quite often, as they got older, she had been left alone with Bryan, when her Mom, and her little brother, would go with their father on his frequent "field trips" when he was a reporter for the highest rated TV station in Seattle. So since they were alone together so often, they had become best friends. When she needed him, he was always there. It was unbelievable that suddenly, their lives were going to change. Already, she could tell, that Malibu was an entirely different world, as different as night and day, to their little town of Moses Lake, Washington. The freeways were bumper to bumper, trendy shops, and fancy restaurants, illuminated by artsy neon signs, lined the busy streets.

Toto, I DO believe we are NOT in Kansas anymore! One thing I'm going to miss about Washington, I know, will be the beautiful trees and the rolling hills leading to nowhere. So far, all I've seen here are buildings, skyscrapers, and industry.

"What do you think? Do I look like a star?" Bryan smiled, giving the best selfie pose he could muster.

Veronica just laughed at her brother, who was sporting his new sunglasses he picked up at their last rest stop. She couldn't deny that her brother was good looking but it got annoying when girls would come up to her just to try and talk to him, with his dark, wavy hair and piercing brown eyes. "Bryan, I think you're getting carried away with this Hollywood thing," she teased tossing her silky, black hair out of her eyes as she maneuvered her midnight blue convertible through the unyielding traffic. Her mind drifted off again as she remembered the day her Dad had called her family, which included, her brothers Bryan, and Tyler, who just turned eight, and her mother Andrea, to tell them they were moving to Los Angeles. Her Dad had just gotten a promotion to station manager for a major local NBC affiliate *KNBC,* which is based out of Burbank, not far from where they were going to live. It never occurred to Veronica that when she started school at Moses Lake High two years ago, she wouldn't be graduating there with the rest of her friends.

"So this is the famous *Pacific Coast Highway.*" Bryan shook his head in awe. All around them was the most breathtakingly beautiful scenery and rock formations they had ever seen. The twisting road curved along the cliffs as the gorgeous Pacific Ocean crashed onto the sparkling sand below.

"Now this is more like it! This is paradise!" Veronica exclaimed. "At least from the way it looks so far, we'll still kind of feel like we're living in the country. I was worried that we would be living right in the heart of the city. Bry, look at those mansions on the cliffs. How can they afford those? Aren't they afraid their homes are going to tumble off the edge?"

"Movie and TV stars live there, no doubt." Bryan concluded, as he switched the radio station. "Our home is going to look just like that. In fact one of those could be ours. Dad's going to be making big bucks at his new position, and with Dad's clout there now, I'm sure he'll be able to get Mom the job she wants as set decorator for *"Days of our Lives!"*

Veronica was so proud that her Mom decided to go back to school to follow her dream to become a set designer. She, out of everyone in the house, was the most excited about moving, since it would put her in the middle of the city where the most interior designers were needed. Their were thousands of studios, and even more TV shows and movie sets where people like her were needed. With a little help from her father, and a friend at *NBC,* she had snagged an interview with the daytime soap.

"If Mom doesn't get that job, there will be hundreds of others she can choose from. Hey, there's the street Dad said to look out for," Bryan pointed. "The next street is ours, *Malibu Canyon Road.*"

"I know, Mom wants that job so bad! She's been watching

that soap for like thirty years," Veronica replied, as she prepared for the turn to their street. "I think her interview is this week sometime. It will be so cool if she gets the job, then I can visit the set anytime I want and meet the cast!"

Bryan turned to his sister. "You just love drama, face it. Do you think you're going to find any mysteries to solve in Malibu? I'm sure there's plenty. This city is famous for- Oh my gosh, what's going on here?"

Bryan stopped in mid-sentence as they turned onto their street. A line of police cars were littered along *Malibu Canyon Road.* Veronica slowed her car to a crawl.

"I hope this isn't our house!"

Bryan shook his head. "No, ours must be farther down. This is #603 and we are #619."

Several officers were surrounding an attractive older woman, who was clearly upset and waving her arms frantically while the officer was taking notes. Out of the crowd, the ultimate California surfer girl came hurrying towards them, with her long, flowing blondish brown hair, Bryan couldn't take his eyes off her.

"Hello, do you guys live around here?" she asked, as she brushed a strand of her hair off her tanned shoulders.

"We're just moving in," Veronica answered, noticing the girl was clearly distraught. "What's going on?"

The girl wiped a tear as it fell down her cheek. "We just got back from a weekend out of town. We were robbed!"

"That's terrible!" Veronica replied, immediately feeling sorry for her. "You don't have an alarm system?"

"The girl shook her head. "We do, but it wasn't turned on. There were no signs of a break-in. We have no idea how they got in. I cannot believe someone just came in and stole all of our stuff! You wouldn't happened to have seen anyone suspicious around here last night?

"No, we just got into town," Bryan stated, holding out his hand. "We're from Washington. I'm Bryan, this is my sister, Veronica."

The girl shook both their hands. "My name is Brittany Sommers. Are you two going to *Malibu High* this Fall?"

"Yes," Veronica smiled. "I'll be a Junior and Bryan's going to be a big Senior."

"That's cool," said Brittany, forcing a smile. I was hoping someone my age would move in that house. It's been vacant for awhile. A lot of people who live on this street are older. If you want, you two can come to our beach party tonight. My best friend is trying to get a bunch of our friends together to help cheer me up."

"That sounds like fun," Veronica accepted as Bryan shook his head in agreement. "Hopefully, we'll get enough unpacked so our parents will let us get away for awhile."

"Great, we're going to meet at *Maria's* restaurant first, to grab a bite to eat, at 6:30pm. It's on *Malibu Pier*."

"That sounds so good right now! I am dying of hunger!" laughed Bryan. "Hopefully, we'll be able to cheer you up."

"Thanks," said Brittany, waving goodbye.

"WOW!" Bryan exclaimed, watching her run up her sloping driveway in his rear view mirror. "I will be in heaven if ALL the girls in Cali look like her!"

"Now Bryan, don't forget about Kristen, aren't you two still together?"

Bryan had met Kristen last year and it had been his first true love. It started out passing notes in Algebra class, as Bryan asked her answers to math problems. Soon after, they started dating and had been together ever since.

Bryan turned to stare at the window. *Thanks a lot, Ronnie, for making me remember what I was trying to not think about. I could have just stayed in Washington and stayed with Kristen, but I know I would be miserable. Knowing that my family was living it up in beautiful California and I was stuck there. It's better this way. I will always love Kristen, if it is true love, I'm sure we will be together someday.*

"So are you two still officially together or not?" Veronica questioned as she slowed the car, still admiring all the beautiful mansions, at least the ones she could see, which were not camouflaged by enormous black iron gates.

Bryan shook his head. "No, we agreed if it was meant to be,

we will find each other again, but we are free to date other people."

"And your happy with that?" Veronica asked with amazement. She had a feeling from the start, that Bryan would be the one to have to adjust the most, but once he got used to it, and maybe met someone new, he would absolutely love it.

"Well it's not like I have a choice," was all he said as they were quiet for the next few minutes, pondering what famous celebrities lived on their street.

"It's not a good sign on the day we move in, someone's house is broken in to," Veronica sighed as they neared the 600 block of their new neighborhood. "Mom and Dad are probably wondering what took us so long!"

"Well, looks like you got your wish, Ronnie," said Bryan, nudging his sister. "Not even in Cali a few hours and already you have a new mystery to solve!"

"I feel so bad for Brittany!" Veronica replied, ignoring her brother's taunts. "I want to help her in any way I can!"

"I knew it!" laughed Bryan as he pointed to a gated driveway entrance that read 619. "Well, home sweet home."

Veronica tried to peer up through the trees on the hill, but could see little. "Look at that, we have our own speaker box that people have to ring outside the gates!" As they climbed the curving driveway, their new house slowly came into view. The mansion was definitely one of the more impressive on the street. Made of black bricks and cobblestone, with sweeping arches and a wide staircase leading up the front patio and entrance. Above the large front doors were enormous bay windows surrounded by a balcony, providing a panoramic view of the rolling green lawns that were accessorized with large rocks and a variety of colorful flowers including bright orange California Poppies.

"I can't believe this!" Veronica cried excitedly, as she maneuvered her convertible behind the moving van, which was backed into the three-car garage. Andrea Chase came out the garage door and waved in enthusiasm upon their arrival.

"It's about time you two got here!" she called, as she mopped her damp forehead. "I thought you were going to follow us on the freeway?"

Veronica hopped out of her car with a sudden burst of energy. "I tried Mom, but Bryan insisted on stopping at the first *In-N-Out Burger* we saw because he wanted to remember the first place he stopped in California."

Bryan smiled and shrugged his broad shoulders as he got his backpack out from the back seat. "What can I say? I've been starving myself for two days so I would have a big appetite for their succulent, juicy burgers!"

Mrs. Chase laughed and shook her head. "Well, let's just hope that meal gave you plenty of energy! There is a lot of hard work and unpacking ahead. I tell you, I'm completely exhausted, and we've only just begun!"

Andrea Chase looked like a classic movie star in every sense of the word, tall and slender, with beautifully expressive eyes, and dark naturally curly hair. Her face was flawlessly perfect, and the animation of her character enchanting. Veronica couldn't get over how her mother still looked as radiant as ever, even after driving fifteen hours.

"We just met a girl on our street who just had her house broken in to," Bryan announced, a concerned look on his handsome face.

Mrs. Chase turned to her daughter with an alarmed look. "What? That's terrible! You would think of all places, this would be a safe neighborhood."

Seconds later, eight year old Tyler came bounding towards them. "Ronnie, Bryan, you're here! Wait till you see my room, it is so cool, this house is awesome!"

Veronica and Bryan laughed at the over-excited enthusiasm of their little brother as he breathlessly told them about their new home.

"This house is so big and there are so many rooms, I got lost twice already! I can't wait to start 'sploring!" Tyler exclaimed, tugging at his older brother's arm. "Bryan, do you wanna go 'sploring?"

Bryan messed up Tyler's brown hair as they walked toward

the house. "First we have a lot of unpacking to do, kiddo. How about we go exploring when it gets dark? I bet all these trees around the house makes it look really spooky at night!"

Suddenly, Tyler's eyes grew big and intrigued. "Do you think there's ghosts living here?"

"Well, if there are any, I'm sure Veronica will do her best to track them down, scare them out, and solve the mystery," Bryan teased as he nudged his sister.

"At least I've found something more productive and rewarding to do than playing video games all day," she replied with a sly smile, who was so used to her brother's teasing that it rarely bothered her anymore. Bryan, however, did not always approve of her constant desire to right wrongs. She often found herself in dangerous situations and he was always the first one to warn her maybe she should take up a new hobby, like reading a book.

"Well, are you guys ready for the grand tour?" asked their mother, as she pulled out another box of dishes from the moving van.

Bryan rushed ahead. "I get first dibs on picking a room!"

As they entered the foyer, Veronica immediately realized their new home was going to be everything she imagined and more. From the warm colors of the dark wooden flooring, to the elegantly crafted moldings and arches in deep jewel tones and rich mahogany, the place looked like a *HGTV Dream Home.* The foyer opened to a massive Great Room which featured large bay windows and a beautiful cobblestone fireplace with large mantle. Off to the right was an open kitchen and dining room. A winding staircase made of dark wood was the centerpiece of the entire home and wound up to a balcony and the bedrooms.

Her father's booming voice floated from the next room. "We were wondering when you two were going to get here! Bryan, get in here and give me a hand!"

They made their way through a maze of boxes to the spacious open Great Room, which was opened to the second floor. The walls all around the room were elegantly inlaid with library boxed woodwork, which made the over-sized room feel homey. Bryan helped his father position the floral-printed couch.

"How do you like it so far?" asked Mr. Chase, with a mischievous smile on his tanned face.

"This is unbelievable, Daddy!" Veronica exclaimed, admiring all the high tech gadgetry by the foyer to monitor the house and the alarm.

Ben Chase was tall and distinguished looking, and still had a decent head of dark hair. With his youthful appearance, many commented he resembled Mike Brady from *"The Brady Bunch."*

Bryan was busy checking out the media center which took up one entire wall. With its big screen 50inch HD smart TV with surround sound, and media/*Blu-ray* player, the room looked like a small movie theater.

Just then, Tyler decided they'd spent enough time gawking at the family room and tried to hurry them along. "Come on," he cried. "You've got to see the game room upstairs!"

Bryan gave in as his brother yanked his arm. "All right, that way I can pick my room before Veronica."

"We're going to have to draw straws or something, Bryan. Besides, I'll be living here longer than you," Veronica called as her brothers hastily made their way up the sweeping staircase. "Mom, how are we ever going to afford this?" she asked, following her into the state of the art kitchen.

"Believe me," Andrea stated as she continued to unload heavily wrapped dishes from boxes. "Your father got a big raise with his promotion, and I hope to get the set designing job with *Days of our Lives.*"

Veronica admired the chrome refrigerator with freezer which opened on bottom rather than top. Large sliding glass doors between the kitchen and the breakfast nook were the entrance to a large outdoor patio and an inviting, interestingly shaped, sparkling pool. Massive rocks surrounded it, and a waterfall splashed down into a lily pond.

"Doesn't that pool make you want to dive in right now?" Mrs Chase asked, as she poured two glasses of lemonade. "Your father ordered coy fish for the pond. Go out and look they are so cute!"

Veronica walked out the glass doors and noticed there was also a Jacuzzi almost hidden by shrubbery near the waterfall and pond. Behind the pool was a lot of overgrown vegetation and as she walked farther back, she could make out a garden area and small cottage.

"Hey, what are you doing out there?" Bryan yelled from above.

Veronica looked up and noticed her brother leaning over a balcony.

"I found my room. It's above the garage right next to the game room. I even have my own entrance and stairs that lead to my front door! You are going to be so jealous! You've got to check out this game room. There's a pool table, two pinball machines, and a video game system. Did we win the lottery or what!?"

"Ronnie, come look at my room!" Tyler shouted excitedly. "I have baseball wallpaper and a bigger bed with my own bathroom!"

"I'll be right up," Veronica called as she made her way back into the house. Her Dad met her as she paused in the breakfast nook to admire the greenhouse windows.

"So what do you think?" he asked running a hand through his wavy, dark hair.

"It feels like a dream, Daddy. This house is every girls dream."

"Well, I figured we worked hard for it. It's important though, to stay humble, and remember where we started. When I was your age my Dad could barely afford to feed us. It takes hard work to get anywhere in life, which is why we didn't just give you and Bryan cars. You saved for those, worked hard, and earned them. I want you to be successful, and follow all your dreams. I just don't want you to take anything for granted."

Veronica shook her head. "I know, Daddy. I'm not going to take any of this for granted."

Mr Chase smiled, and kissed his daughter on the forehead. "I love you, pumpkin."

"I love you too, Daddy."

Just then, Bryan called from the top of the stairs. "Hello, Miss Veronica, we're waiting for you."

"Where's Woody?" asked Veronica as she made her way up the stairs. I hope he's not scared because of the move. Their fluffy, orange and white Maine Coon cat was the best pet Veronica ever had. He was always affectionate and liked to lick your fingers. He was like a dog and loved to fetch rolled up balls of newspaper.

"He did fine in our cat carrier," her Mom called from the kitchen. "He meowed a lot, but I kept talking to him and after awhile he calmed down. He's upstairs in your room. I figured he should get used to it first."

"My room?" questioned Veronica. "How did my room get selected for me?" She reached the top of the stairs and heard her brothers had already hooked up video games. She poked her head in and realized it was the game room.

"Did you see my room?" Tyler asked as he pounded on his video game controller.

"I'm getting there," Veronica replied. "But first I want to see my room and check on Woody." She turned and walked down the hallway towards the door at the end. When she opened the door she immediately fell in love with the cozy room. Two French doors led out to a balcony which overlooked the pool and the grounds. Her cat was peacefully sleeping in his comfy bed in the corner of the room which was filled with nothing but boxes. She discovered she had her own bathroom with marble bathtub/shower and a vanity big enough to fit four people, plus a spacious walk-in closet. *I must be one of the luckiest girls in the world right now!* Veronica thought, her mind racing with ideas on how she wanted to decorate her bathroom. Her Mother's voice calling from downstairs interrupted her thoughts.

"These boxes aren't going to get unloaded by themselves!" she called. "Let's go you guys!"

Three hours later, Veronica was lying on her comfy bed, un-open boxes still surrounded her, but she was too exhausted to move.

"Hey, Ronnie," Bryan called peeping his head in her room.

"It's almost 6 o'clock, we need to leave if we're going to meet Brittany at *Maria's*."

"Oh my gosh, I totally lost track of time," Veronica exclaimed, practically leaping from the bed. "I need to find the box with all my clothes and take a quick shower."

"Good luck in finding anything in this disaster!" Bryan laughed. "I'll meet you downstairs in fifteen minutes."

****　　　　****　　　　****

"I can't wait for the movers to bring my Jeep," said Bryan as they cruised down *Pacific Coast Highway* twenty minutes later.

"Are you tired of being driven around already?" asked Veronica, feeling refreshed in her white and blue printed spaghetti strapped summer dress.

"Very. Driving in your car will definitely ensure that I don't see my graduation next June."

"Bryan, it's so weird that we're living right on the ocean," Veronica continued, ignoring her brother's comment. "I didn't get a chance to go far into the backyard but from what I could tell, I'm sure we have a gorgeous view of the ocean."

"I checked it out. You can fully see the waves crashing onto the rocks from the edge of our property. We are so lucky, Ronnie. I just hope we can make some good friends like we had back home. I hope they're not all phony and superficial like they say everyone in L.A is."

"Well, if Brittany is any example, I'm sure we'll have friends in no time. She seems really nice."

After a few minutes, they finally found a spot in the crowded *Malibu Pier* parking lot. The Pier was a long strip of shops and restaurants that hovered above the sparkling ocean. Many of the restaurants had balconies that offered spectacular views of the beach and the crashing waves.

"This is definitely a tourist hot spot," Bryan commented as he hopped out of the car. "I can't wait to learn how to surf. I've always wanted to do that."

"If you want to be out there with all those sharks be my

guest. Haven't you heard the reports on how sharks seem to be attacking humans more often these days? I saw a *Discovery Channel* special where they were leaping out of the water like dolphins."

Bryan laughed as they headed for the Pier. "Ronnie, I think you've been watching too much television and *JAWS* re-runs."

"OK, don't say I didn't warn you."

The late June sun was setting and creating magnificent sparkles which danced on the ocean. A few remaining surfers were still riding the waves. Veronica and Bryan made their way down *Malibu Pier* which was still bustling with people of all ages, shopping or just hanging out.

"Smell that sea air? This is what I've been longing for! Hey, there's *Maria's,*" pointed Bryan. "I am starving and Mexican food will definitely hit the spot."

They entered the cozy cafe adorned with beautiful Mexican artifacts and colorful tapestries.

"Veronica, over here," called Brittany from a table in the corner.

Veronica could tell already her new friend was still upset over the burglary at her home.

"Glad you two could make it," she said with a smile. "This is Veronica, and- oops I forgot..."

"Bryan," he finished, extending his hand to Brittany's two friends.

"They just moved from Washington and they're both going to *Malibu High*," Brittany continued. "This is my boyfriend, Carlos, and my best friend, Aja. Carlos' Mom is the owner of this cafe. I can't wait for you to meet her, she is the coolest!"

Veronica shook hands with both as they sat down in the booth. Surveying the group, she immediately felt like she was part of some reality show, everyone was good looking. Brittany was the typical California girl, with silky blondish-brown hair. Carlos was very Latino, with smooth skin and dark, close cropped hair, shaved on the sides, and a goatee on his chin. Aja had flowing, reddish-auburn hair, and appeared to be wearing little make-up, but still looked beautiful. Veronica already sensed she would love her new friends. "So, how's everything going, Brittany? Have the police found any leads on who might have done this?"

Brittany shook her head. "None. But I've already told the police who I suspect."

"Who?" Veronica asked, helping herself to a chip with salsa.

"Well, my Mom decided she is going to re-marry, she informed me of this two weeks ago. She's marrying a guy she met online. He has a son our age, Josh Townsend, who came with his Dad to our house for dinner last weekend. He plays guitar and I guess he has a band. I *know* he has something to do with this. My Mom stupidly gave his Dad a key the house. I have a feeling Josh had it duplicated and came in and ripped us off!"

Carlos shook his head as he took a drink of *Coke*. "I can't believe Josh had anything to do with this," he commented, loading up another chip of his Mom's freshly made house salsa. "Believe me, I know him. We've hung out a few times. Yes, he's had his problems, his Mom was killed in a car accident when Josh was two. He lives in a bad part of L.A and grew up with the wrong crowd. Now that Josh's Dad is living more at Brittany's with her Mom, Josh will be going to *Malibu High*."

"I bet he and his friends came in and stole everything so they could sell it," Brittany continued, turning to Aja for affirmation.

"I think you're just upset your Mom's re-marrying, baby," Carlos said, running a hand along her back. "You're just going out of your way to think up wild thoughts about Josh and his Dad."

"How long have you known Josh?" Veronica questioned, wondering why Brittany was so sure he was behind the burglary.

"I just met him about two weeks ago, when my Mom decided it was time to introduce us since they were suddenly engaged. So far, his Dad has been cool with me," Brittany replied, suddenly noticing Aja was finding it hard to keep her eyes off Bryan as much as she was. "But enough about that, isn't this salsa addictive? Maria makes it from scratch daily. I've begged her to give me the recipe but she refuses. By the way, where is your Mom, Carlos? I haven't seen her since we got here. She usually comes out to greet us by now."

Carlos shook his head, scanning the crowded cafe. "We're really busy right now, she's probably helping out in the kitchen. She is looking for a new manager and wants to cut back on working. I'd better go see if she needs anything," he said, getting up from the booth and giving Brittany a kiss on the cheek.

"You are so lucky!" Aja smiled, watching as Carlos headed for the kitchen. "He is so gorgeous and so good to you. I wish I could find someone like that!"

Brittany rolled her eyes. "Please, Aja. You are so beautiful. The reason you're not with anyone is cause you're too shy and guys are intimidated to ask you out. Wouldn't you be intimidated to ask her out, Bryan?"

"Actually, no." Bryan replied with a grin. "So Aja, do you want to go out sometime?"

"Bryan, I can't believe you!" Veronica exclaimed, pushing her brother so that he nearly fell out of the booth.

Suddenly, Brittany's face went white as she noticed someone come through the front door of *Maria's.*

"Brittany, you look like you've seen a ghost!" noticed Veronica, turning to see what she was looking at.

"It's Josh," Brittany announced, trying not to catch his eye, "and he's coming this way!"

2

Clue in
the Bonfire

"Speak of the devil," Brittany exclaimed. "Before long, when he officially moves in, I'll be seeing enough of him at home!"

Josh strolled in the cafe, with his friend, causing many people to turn and look as they came in. Josh was carrying his guitar across his back and as he noticed Brittany, he made his way over. Veronica watched him closely, wondering if he really was behind the burglary. She couldn't see him ripping off Brittany's home. He was wearing a white tank top and blue jeans. His hair was dark, and fell down into his dark, brown eyes. His face was smooth and tanned. She noticed he was looking directly at her, as if waiting for an introduction, then he suddenly diverted his attention back to Brittany.

"I heard what happened," he said, with genuine sympathy in his voice. "That sucks. My Dad is pretty pissed about the whole thing."

"Yeah, it's pretty upsetting," Brittany agreed nonchalantly. "But they'll eventually catch whoever's behind this."

"By the way, this is Jimmy, I'm sure you've seen him at school," Josh continued introducing his friend.

"Hey, I remember you from math class!" said Jimmy to Aja. "Thanks for sitting by me. If you weren't in the class I'd probably gotten an "F!"

Aja laughed. "Yeah, I'm glad you learned so much by copying off my paper!"

"This is Veronica and her brother, Bryan. They just moved here from Washington," said Brittany, knowing that was what Josh was waiting for. "So, what did you do this weekend while we were out of town?"

"We just kicked it at Zuma," Josh replied. "Hey, I heard you're having a beach party tonight. Do you mind if me and Jimmy come? I wanted to play you guys a song I've been working on to see what you think."

"What's up, Josh?" Carlos exclaimed as he returned to the table with menus. "You coming to our little get-together tonight?"

Josh nodded. "Yeah, of course we'll be there! I'll bring something good for us to drink."

"Cool," Carlos replied, as he handed everyone at the table menus. "We should be down there in a couple of hours."

"Sounds good," said Josh as he turned to Brittany. "Don't worry about what happened," he stated, resting a hand on her shoulder. "I'll do everything I can to help track down whoever's behind this and get all your stuff back."

Brittany rolled her eyes as Josh and his friend sat in the booth in front of them. "He has a lot of nerve!" she whispered, angry that Carlos invited him after she just told him how she felt. "He's practically flaunting in my face that he stole everything! Carlos, why did you invite him?"

"Brittany, are you going to take my word that I know Josh wouldn't do anything like that? I don't know why you keep going on and on about this. He's a good guy, you don't even know him."

Brittany felt her face redden at Carlos' outburst. Lately, she began to question whether Carlos was even right for her. He had been acting strange lately. He seemed to lose his temper more frequently, and had become very controlling. *I honestly don't know how much more I can take.* "I need some air." Brittany stated as she abruptly got up from the booth and made her way towards the front entrance.

Carlos was about to go after her when he realized he'd better wait and let her cool down. "Sorry, about that," he said turning back towards the group. "I just don't get why she even thinks Josh is behind this. I think it's because he soon will be her step-brother and she can't stand it. Anyways, we're a little short staffed today, so I'll be your waiter. What can I get for you, Veronica?"

"I'll have two tacos and an enchilada #2," Veronica stated, closing her menu. "That sounds really good."

"And I'll have #4," said Bryan, taking another chip with a heap of salsa.

Veronica turned to her brother with a smile. "How did I know you were going to order that!"

"That's my Mom's specialty," Carlos grinned. "I usually get that myself. It's very filling. A macho chicken burrito, with white rice and black beans."

"So how is everyone doing today?" asked a plump, older woman, with a strong Spanish accent, who Veronica immediately realized must be Carlos' mother, Maria.

"Mrs. Gutierrez! How are you doing?" smiled Aja. "I want you to meet some new friends. They just moved here from Washington. Veronica and Bryan."

"So nice to meet you!" Maria exclaimed extending her hand. "My, you are truly *bonita*," commented Maria, admiring her dark hair and complexion. "You would look right at home in one of my beautiful Spanish dresses."

"Thank you!" Veronica smiled, her face reddening.

"Oh my gosh, Maria," Bryan laughed. "Let's not give Veronica a bigger ego than she already has!"

"Don't listen to him," Veronica interjected. "He's just jealous I am the best looking in the family! By the way, I love your cafe, and the salsa is to die for!"

Maria's smile faded. "Thank you, but I'm sure Carlos told you the news. It's quite upsetting."

Veronica gave Aja a look. "What news?"

Maria turned towards her son with surprise. "Carlos didn't tell you?"

"Sorry, I didn't want to give you any more bad news," her son shrugged.

"What is it, Maria?" asked Aja, realizing something must be really wrong for Maria to look so unhappy.

"They may have to tear down the Pier," Maria stated, her voice breaking.

"What?" Veronica and Aja looked at each other in shock.

"Well, apparently the city did some tests and they found the Pier needs some major renovations structurally for it to be up to code," Maria continued, brushing a wayward strand of hair out of her eyes. "The cost is astronomical. More than any of us merchants could afford and stay in business. So we may have to close."

"That's terrible!" Aja exclaimed, immediately feeling sorry for Maria. "It just wouldn't be the same without you here, the whole Pier for that matter!"

"There must be something we can do," Veronica stated turning towards her brother.

"It's quite doubtful we're going to be able to do anything," Maria replied sadly, as she surveyed the cafe. She and Carlos had sacrificed a lot to open the restaurant. It had been a long time dream, but after years of hard work and saving, they had finally reached their goal. Now it appeared, everything could be lost. "Unfortunately, it's up to the city," Maria continued. "If we can't come up with the money, we'll have to close down. But listen, enough about that! Tonight dinner is on me. It will be my welcome to California gift to both of you."

"Thank you, Maria!" Bryan exclaimed. "I can't wait to try your food. I know I'll love it!"

Maria smiled in spite of everything. "I'll talk to you all before you leave. I need to get back to the kitchen." With that, she turned and stopped to check on another table.

"I swear, when it rains it pours!" Bryan sighed, looking out the window at the gorgeous view of the ocean.

"Maria will be so upset if she has to close down," said Aja turning to Carlos. "I can't believe you didn't tell us about this."

"I'm sure they won't tear down the Pier," Carlos stated as he took the menus from Veronica and Bryan. "This is a popular tourist attraction. They'll figure out something."

"Well, you sound more confident than your Mom," said Bryan matter-of -factly.

"It will all be fine," Carlos assured them. "So Aja, what can I get for you?"

"I'll have the same as Veronica," Aja replied, looking towards the front entrance for Brittany.

"Coming up!" Carlos said as he gathered up the menus. "I'll be back. I'm going to go talk to Brittany."

Brittany sat on a bench on the Pier and looked out at the beach and the crashing waves. The sun was setting and it was dancing on the ocean. The sky was a beautiful purple and orange. A cool breeze was tickling her face. As much as she didn't want to believe it, it seemed everything was falling apart. All their belongings were stolen, her Mom was getting married, they would be all living together, and that included living with Josh. *And to top it off, my boyfriend doesn't believe me when I tell him anything.* Brittany remembered how great it was when she and Carlos first got together. They met in Spanish and he offered to tutor since he was familiar with the language. Before long, they were going out. Carlos was her first serious boyfriend and the first guy she ever slept with. Everything seemed so right, she thought they would eventually get married, but now she wasn't sure.

A sound behind her snapped Brittany back to the present. She whirled around and saw Carlos standing nearby. *How long had he been standing there?*

"What are you thinking about?" Carlos questioned, as he made his way over to her. "I'm sorry I snapped at you," he whispered, forcing her to look at him. "You know Josh is one of my good friends. Of course I'm going to stick up for him. Just give him a break, OK? Remember don't accuse anyone until you have some proof. Have you forgotten, innocent until proven guilty?"

There was a silence that broke between them.

"I love you so much, Brittany. I hate when we fight."

"Believe me, I hate it too," Brittany replied, feeling her eyes become watery.

Carlos moved his face closer to hers and they hugged. She couldn't deny her feelings for him were still very strong. "Come on, we'd better get back, your dinner is probably cold by now."

****   ****   ****

An hour later, the group was waving goodbye and thank yous to Maria as they got up from the booth.

Brittany hurried passed Josh's table as Carlos stopped.

"We'll see you down there in a few," Josh stated to Carlos as he fixed himself another grilled steak fajita. "That new girl is pretty hot, bro!" Josh turned to look again at Veronica as they were talking near the front entrance.

"Yeah, she and her brother are pretty cool!" Carlos grinned. "I'm going to get changed and I'll meet you down there." They gave each other their usual fist bump as Carlos returned to the group. "I just need to help clean up around here a little. I'll meet you at Paradise Cove in a few."

"All right," Brittany replied, as they headed out the front entrance.

They exited the cafe and immediately felt the warmth of the late June evening, which wasn't as bad than in the city.

"I swear, that was the best Mexican food I've ever had!" Bryan announced emphatically, rubbing his stomach.

"I'm surprised you like any other Mexican food besides *Taco Bell!*" laughed Veronica as they made there way down *Malibu Pier.* "You practically live there!"

"Actually, I prefer *Del Taco,*" Bryan answered, enjoying the fresh sea air and the warm wind blowing against his face.

It was nearing 9pm and the crowd on the Pier was dissipating.

"I still can't believe they might tear the Pier down!" Aja exclaimed, as they walked down the wooden steps towards the beach.

"I've got it!" Veronica exclaimed as she stopped in her tracks.

"Got what?" Bryan asked, knowing when his sister had a brainstorm as suddenly as this one, it meant he would have to help her out in some way.

"We could have a beach benefit to raise money to save the Pier!"

"That sounds like a great idea, Veronica!" Aja agreed. "Like a carnival on the beach! We could charge admission, maybe we could ask some local bands to play at the carnival, and set up game booths, ask merchants for donations, maybe find a way to get rides, we could raise a lot of money!"

"Hey, maybe we could ask some celebrities who live in Malibu for donations!" Brittany reasoned.

Bryan put his hand to his chin. "Ronnie, you never cease to amaze me, you're always coming up with great, but outlandish ideas!"

"We'll have to make plans fast," Veronica continued, ignoring her brother. "We don't have much time to come up with the money, according to Maria."

"Tomorrow, bright and early, we'll have to get together and start making calls and see who we can get to participate in this," said Brittany.

"Perfect idea!" Veronica agreed, her mind already racing with ideas.

"I could go for a swim!" Bryan said, wiping his forehead.

Aja grabbed her keys from her Gucci bag. "I'm going to run to the car and get the cooler and stuff to make s'mores."

"Mmmm, that sounds good! Need a hand?" offered Bryan.

"Sure," Aja replied. "We'll meet you at the cove in a few minutes," she said as Brittany and Veronica continued down the sandy beach.

"OK," said Brittany, looking back to give Aja a sly smile as she and Bryan headed for the parking lot. "Your brother is so cute! If I wasn't with anyone I would go for him in a heartbeat!"

"Believe me, he is well aware of it! He's a cool brother though. I can't imagine where I'd be without him," said Veronica, her hair blowing in the refreshing breeze.

"I think Aja has a crush on him already! Did you see those two? They were eyeing each other the entire time we were at *Maria's*."

"That's Bryan," Veronica replied with a sigh. "I doubt though he will get in any serious relationships anytime soon. He was going out with a girl in Washington for awhile. I know he really loves her."

They were silent for awhile while they continued down the beach, listening as the massive waves crashed all around them. Veronica found it hard to believe she was actually in California, walking on a beautiful beach, when just yesterday she was in Washington facing another cloudy, dull day.

Brittany broke the silence. "Veronica, I am so glad you moved here. It's cool having another friend to talk to. Things have been crazy the last few days."

"I'm glad to," Veronica replied as they reached Paradise Cove.

She realized why everyone liked to hang out here. The area was secluded by rock formations on all sides. This was obviously the best place to party because no one could be spotted from *Pacific Coast Highway* high above them.

Brittany brought out a beach blanket from her bag and laid it out on the sand. "I wish Carlos hadn't invited Josh. I need to talk with my Mom and tell her what I suspect."

"Have they set a date for the wedding?" asked Veronica, as they all arranged their blankets.

"It's supposed to be on New Year's Eve." Brittany replied, popping open a can of *Diet Coke.* "My Mom has been interviewing wedding planners, and can't seem to find one she likes. It's going to be a big elaborate, very expensive event!"

"Oh, that will be so beautiful!" Veronica exclaimed, as she began writing messages in the sand with a stick. "So, tell me more about Josh. I don't get why you think he did it."

"He hangs with losers like his friend Jimmy who is always getting into trouble at school. Last May, they found a bike outside Josh's apartment stolen from school. When they questioned him, he said the guy who owned it gave him permission but the owner denied doing so. I mean, why was the bike in front of his house?"

"Does anyone else have access to your house?" Veronica asked, doubting the burglary was actually committed by someone she knew.

Brittany thought for a minute. "Well, there's our maid, Jeanette, but she certainly isn't capable of ripping us off. They took all our electronics, including our 50 inch TV, an iPad, two computers, some expensive vases and paintings, plus a lot of my Mom's expensive jewelry which is irreplaceable."

"Well, one thing I've learned these days," Veronica stated, "Is that anyone can commit a crime. No one should be ruled out."

****   ****   ****

"So, I still can't believe you're not with anyone," said Bryan as he and Aja reached the sand of the beach with the supplies, and headed down the steep, winding path to the cove below.

"Oh, believe me, I've had offers, but none from anyone I'm really interested in. So what about you? Did you break someone's heart when you left Washington?"

Bryan was silent for a moment. "Yeah, I did. Her name is Kristen. We were so good together. We kind of knew our Dad was going to get the job months in advance, so we were prepared for it. It didn't make it any less difficult saying goodbye though. Do you live in Malibu?"

"Actually, I live on the same street as you and Brittany. It's cool we all live so close. We can have a lot of sleep-overs!"

"I've heard the *Santa Monica Pier* is cool too," Bryan exclaimed. "I heard they have some really good rides. Maybe you could show it to me sometime."

"That would be fun! My family owns a restaurant just off that Pier." Aja smiled as they reached the cove and spotted Brittany and Veronica.

"Oh that's cool! Another friend who owns a restaurant," Bryan said happily, realizing he will need to step up his work-out routine.

The sun had completely set and it was getting dark. The beach was virtually deserted and the only sound was the violent crashing of the waves.

"We'd better get that campfire started," Bryan stated as they re-joined their friends and helped unload the bags.

Aja greeted her brother, Nalu, who just arrived and she introduced him to everyone. He was Hawaiian looking like Aja, and typically had spiky dark hair, but lately he had been dying his hair different colors, and this week it was blue.

Another group was heading towards them from the opposite direction, and Aja recognized one of them to be Josh. He appeared suddenly with Carlos and Jimmy.

"We brought some refreshments," Josh announced, taking a long swig of one in his hand. "Who wants one?"

Brittany gave Josh an evil look as she got up and walked towards the water.

Josh's smile faded as he watched her leave.

"She's just really emotional right now," Carlos reasoned as he placed two six packs in the cooler. "Come on, let's find some driftwood so we can start the fire."

"I'm going to go see if Brittany is OK," said Veronica, getting up to follow her friend. *There has to be some other reason why she feels so strongly Josh is behind this.* Veronica thought, as she headed towards the water. *From what I've seen of him so far, he doesn't look like a thief at all. That whole bike stealing situation sounds like it was just a misunderstanding. I wonder if she just resents the fact that her Mom is getting married again and is looking for an excuse to give her so she won't. I'll have to remember to ask what happened to her Dad.*

Bryan found a large piece of driftwood and laid it in the pit. "Look's like this is a popular spot for campfires, someone had one here not too long ago. So, what's fun to do around here?" Bryan asked Nalu, as they walked together to find more firewood.

"I just got certified as a scuba instructor. I love it!"

"Scuba diving! I've always wanted to do that! Ever since I saw *Titanic* I've been interesting in exploring for lost ships, and it's so fascinating to see all those underwater photos of the actual ship. It's a trip after all these years, the water still preserved a lot of the artifacts. There's a whole other world down there!"

"Yeah, I could spend all day admiring all the beautiful, exotic fish. I want Aja to take the class but she is too afraid for some reason the oxygen tank would break on her."

"I know they show you how to fully test your gear to make sure that doesn't happen," Bryan replied, as he pulled another log out from between two rocks. "I'm sure Veronica would take the class too."

****   ****   ****

Veronica reached Brittany who was sitting in the sand, watching the waves as they washed up the beach not far from her.

"I can't believe Carlos would invite him, AND show up with him," said Brittany, glancing back at the group who was listening to Josh, as he started playing his guitar. "I mean, look at him, he doesn't even care how I feel. He knows something's wrong."

"Maybe he truly believes Josh wouldn't rob you and he doesn't want him to feel left out," Veronica offered, suddenly feeling a chill as the air grew colder.

"You know what, I'm not even going to trip about it. I'll find out sooner or later if Josh really is behind this. In fact, I'm going to find out tonight! Come on!"

Brittany got up and hurried back to the party. The boys had the fire blazing and they were kicking back around it as Josh was playing guitar, the melody was enchanting. Shadows were dancing on their tanned faces as Aja and Bryan were preparing marshmallows and chocolate for the s'mores.

Carlos put his arm around Brittany as she and Veronica returned to the group. "Are you OK, baby?" he asked, pulling her close.

Brittany nodded and pulled away. "Let's play a game," she exclaimed, grabbing a beer from the cooler and popping it open. "Let's play Truth or Dare." She watched for Josh's reaction, wondering if he was going to try and suggest something else so he wouldn't have to reveal anything.

"That sounds cool," Jimmy replied. "You can pick me first cause I have a good dare for Aja," he smirked, eyeing her mischievously.

"And how do you know I'll even pick dare?" she asked as she roasted two marshmallows on her poker stick.

"Let's see," Brittany continued, not wanting to pick Josh right off the bat. "Aja, Truth or Dare?"

Aja glanced at Bryan as the boys chanted "Dare! Dare!"

"Truth," Aja replied, giving them a "so there" look.

"Is it true that you are attracted to someone in this group?" Brittany questioned, already anticipating the answer.

Aja paused, as if unsure what she should say. Then finally, "Yes, I'll have to say yes," she stated as everyone made catcalls and whistled.

"I know it's me," Jimmy announced. "You can admit it."

"I'm not saying another word," Aja smiled as she pushed the marshmallows and chocolate together between her two graham crackers. "My lips are sealed!"

Bryan watched her intently as he prepared another s'more, wondering if it was him.

"OK, your turn to ask, Aja," said Brittany, taking another sip of her beer.

"Let's see," Aja began, deciding on who she wanted to pick. "Jimmy, Truth or Dare?"

"Dare!" Jimmy replied, rubbing his hands together in anticipation.

"Get him back for copying from your paper all those times, girl!" Brittany laughed, obviously getting tipsy. Carlos gave her a disapproving look as he grabbed another from the cooler.

Aja thought for a moment. "OK, I dare you to strip and do a dance for us in the ocean!"

"What?!" Jimmy exclaimed as the girls in the group laughed and clapped.

"You have to do it!" Brittany stated, "Or the next one will be worse!"

Jimmy shrugged. "I have no problem with it," he said, jogging towards the ocean and pulling down his surfer shorts. He made his way into the water and began dancing and moving like he was a member of a boy band.

"Love the underwear!" Brittany laughed as the boys whistled.

"Don't do that anymore, Jimmy!" Nalu teased. "You're going to make me want to ask you out!"

Jimmy grabbed his shorts and pulled them up. "Don't worry, it's all good, I guess you deserved that show for helping me out so much in math. So now it's MY turn to ask! Josh, Truth or Dare?"

"Dare!" Josh replied, knowing Jimmy would give him something good.

"OK. I dare you to take Veronica and show her why they call this spot Paradise Cove!" Jimmy smiled, giving Josh a knowing look.

Josh grinned and looked at Veronica. "You don't have to if you don't want to," he said as he got up and placed his guitar gently on the blanket.

"It's OK," Veronica replied. "A dare is a dare."

"OK, well, we'll be right back," Josh announced as they walked farther back into the dark cove.

"You two have fun!" Jimmy called as they disappeared into the darkness of the mountainous rocks.

Here is my chance to find out more information about him! Veronica thought as she followed him through a maze of rock formations. *I still can't imagine him ripping off Brittany's home. He seems so sweet, but he does put up a front around his buddies.*

"You're going to love this spot," Josh continued, as he

grabbed her hand. They made their way along a ledge of rock, until they reached a small opening that looked like an entrance to a cave, but was actually a path which they followed. The only sound was the crashing of the ocean in the distance.

Maybe this wasn't such a good idea, Veronica. she thought. *I barely know him, what is he expecting we're going to do? I'm too trusting, but I don't know what it is, I feel comfortable and almost safe with him.*

Soon, they found themselves surrounded by a beautiful lagoon. The nearly full moon, which was directly above them, cast enough light to illuminate the crystal blue waters that were gently tapping the rocks around them. Ledges surrounded the lagoon and a flat rock in the center created a perfect bench for them to sit. Veronica placed her flip flops on the rock and they both put there legs in the semi-warm water.

"So, what do you think?" Josh whispered, staring directly into her eyes.

Veronica couldn't escape his deep, brown eyes as they connected. "It's really beautiful," she managed to say, feeling her pulse racing.

"I'm glad we got a chance to be alone," he continued. "I've been wanting to tell you something."

"What is it?" Veronica asked. Her mind racing with questions she wanted to ask him.

He continued to stare at her intensely. "It's just when I first saw you at *Maria's,* I couldn't keep my eyes off you. I was totally drawn to you," he said, finding it hard to put into words how he was feeling. "I would really like to get to know you better. I was thinking it would be cool for all of us to go out for a bite at this awesome restaurant called *Luau Island.* Aja and Nalu's parents actually own it. We could ask everyone to join."

"That sounds cool," Veronica agreed, trying to read his eyes for clues. *My initial feeling about him was right! I'm sure he didn't commit the robbery. I just can't see him doing that.*

"We better get back," he said interrupting her thoughts. "They are going to start wondering what we are up to!"

They made their way along the path, to the cave opening. As they came out, they realized a dense, misty fog had suddenly materialized out of nowhere.

"Wow," Veronica exclaimed. "This beach can be really spooky at night!"

Just then, a ghostly figure appeared out of the fog, causing them both to jump with a start. Veronica's heart leaped out of her chest but calmed down when she realized it was her brother.

"Bryan, you scared us to death!" Veronica shrieked, trying to rub the goosebumps from her arms.

"I was beginning to worry about you!" he stated, eyeing Josh suspiciously.

"Hey," Josh interjected. "We are trying to get a group together to go to this cool restaurant called *Luau Island* in Santa Monica. My friend owns it and we can get a great discount!"

"That sounds good," Bryan agreed as they returned to the group. The fire had died down, and everyone was huddled together under blankets to keep warm.

Josh picked up his guitar and started playing a soft relaxing melody. Veronica took a seat on the blanket next to him as he started singing. He had a great voice and was very talented.

The night air seemed to grow colder by the minute, and the fog cast an eerie, ghostly mist over all of them. As Josh finished the song everyone clapped.

Suddenly, Aja noticed someone's old DVDs had fallen in the bonfire. What's this?" she asked, reaching for one that only semi-burned. "Did someone accidentally drop these into the fire?"

"What is it?" Brittany slurred, almost falling over as she got up.

"It's a DVD," Aja replied.

Half of it was completely melted but the other half remained untouched by the fire. "I guess they didn't like the movie," Aja joked, trying to read what was written in magic marker on front of the disc. "*Disneyland* trip---"

Suddenly, Brittany snatched it out of her hand. "Oh my gosh! This is a video of our vacation last month! It was in our *Blu-*

ray player that was stolen!" she shrieked, as the fog swirled around them and the air suddenly turned to ice.

3

The Missing Necklace

Brittany stared at the disc in shock, still not believing it was their homemade DVD from a summer vacation trip, which was in the stolen player. "Whoever ripped us off, tried to destroy the evidence in the bonfire!" she stated, as Carlos came over to give her support.

Aja felt a cold shiver crawl down her spine. "I can't believe they did that! Those memories can never be recaptured. I hope you have a back-up!"

"Well, it's obvious whoever broke in your house comes here and knows this place," Bryan reasoned, turning to glance at the group.

Brittany nodded. "Yeah, and this confirms who I've suspected all along! I've got to get out of here. This place creeps me out!" She got up abruptly and started gathering her things as Veronica and Aja helped, and the boys started talking about plans for the following evening. Brittany glanced back at them, and then turned to her friends. "I am more convinced than ever Josh is behind this!" She whispered. "He hangs out here all the time. What were you two doing so long in the cave?" she asked Veronica with a knowing smile.

"Oh, we were just talking. He showed me the lagoon," Veronica replied. "He invited us out tomorrow night to *Luau Island.* I was thinking we could try and get more information out of him. *And maybe you will see who he truly is and realize he has nothing to do with this.*

"That's my family's restaurant!" Aja exclaimed. "You will love the atmosphere, it's filled with tons of tropical plants and flowers; the whole experience is like a Hawaiian luau."

"That sounds nice!" Veronica replied, hoping her Mom and Dad would let them go out another night so soon after moving in.

Brittany thought it over for a moment then a smile broke across her face. "Actually that's perfect! I have an idea. By tomorrow night we should be able to find out who is behind this when we bust him as he's breaking into another house!"

"How are we going to do that?" Aja questioned, glancing back at the boys.

"I can't explain it now. I'll give you all the details tomorrow," Brittany promised, as the group made their way up the dark dirt path towards the Pier parking lot.

**** **** ****

It was nearing midnight as Veronica and Bryan headed down *Pacific Coast Highway* for home.

"What a day!" Bryan exclaimed, stretching back in the plush seat. "So, what did you and Josh do for so long?"

"We were just talking. I'll have to show you the lagoon sometime. It's really a beautiful spot. Looks like you and Aja really hit it off. I think she has a crush on you!"

"Why do you think that?" Bryan questioned, eyeing his sister. "Did she tell you something?"

"No, I can tell, that's all."

"She's a cool girl, but I don't think she's really my type. She seems a little reserved and quiet, but I wouldn't mind getting to know her better. Tomorrow should be fun. I am going to sleep like a log tonight!"

"We're going to have to get up extra early to finish unpacking if we're going to meet everyone at noon to start planning the benefit carnival. I'm going to ask Daddy if he can arrange a news story on *KNBC* about the Pier so we can get donations and publicity for the event."

"Good idea. I'm sure Dad can swing it, but we don't have a lot of time if we're going to have it on Saturday."

"Well, with all of us working on it, I know we can pull it off. The main thing is to get permission to have the carnival on the beach."

They were silent for the next few minutes as they started down *PCH.* Bryan was about to close his eyes and rest, when he spotted a moving van parked on the side of the cliffs near *Paradise Cove.* No one seemed to be in or around it. "That's strange," he commented, hoping the driver hadn't run out of gas and was walking.

Veronica slowed the car as they came up on it. "Wouldn't it be a trip if all Brittany's things were in that truck? We better check it out!"

"We can't just walk up on the truck" Bryan reasoned. "They may have pulled over to sleep for the night."

Veronica got out of the car and peered into the truck cab. It was empty, except for fast food containers and cups. She noticed the truck was parked near the access trail that went straight to *Paradise Cove.* She wished she could investigate further, but knew her brother would not stand for it.

For the rest of the ride home, Veronica tried to put all the pieces of the puzzle together. *I definitely need another clue before I can get a handle on this mystery! Obviously, the thief was on the beach and was trying to destroy the evidence of the burned DVDs.* The more she thought about it, the more she suspected the moving van was somehow tied to the burglaries. *I think I should ask Brittany's neighbors if they saw a moving van outside her residence.* Veronica looked over at her brother and noticed he had fallen asleep. She knew she was about to do just that when her head hit her pillow!

**** **** ****

The next morning at breakfast, Veronica and Bryan filled their parents in on everything that had happened.

"It sounds like you've made some good friends already," said Mr. Chase, as he took a sip of coffee.

"Dad, do you think you could set up a news segment piece on the possible closure of the Pier and the Benefit?" Bryan asked, taking another bite of sausage and bacon.

"That shouldn't be a problem," he replied. "I can get a crew out tomorrow to get footage of the Pier and some interviews."

"I want to help with the carny-ville!" Tyler announced, between spoonfuls of cereal.

"You can help me build the booths," Bryan offered, giving his little brother a wink.

"Can I Mom?" he asked excitedly.

"We'll see," Mrs. Chase replied. "We still have a lot to do around here. I want you two to fully unpack your rooms before you go anywhere today," she said to Veronica and Bryan.

They finished eating their scrumptious breakfast of blueberry pancakes, bacon, sausage, cereal, and bagels. Since they rarely had a chance to sit down together, they made it a point to do so for breakfast or lunch on Sundays. Mrs Chase usually made pasta for lunch on Sundays with her famous spicy red sauce, that was a recipe passed down in the family for generations.

For the next several hours, Veronica finished unpacking seemingly endless numbers of boxes. *I swear, I never imagined I had so much stuff!* Veronica thought as she came across a box that held numerous pictures she still needed to put into albums. Her eye caught a photo that was on top of the stack, and she picked it up. It was a photo of her first boyfriend, Erik, whom she met when she was a Sophomore at Moses Lake High six months ago. She remembered how, at first, she really thought she was in love, but now she realized what it all really amounted to; an infatuation, a desire to be in a relationship and to experience the feeling of truly being in love. Erik was the star quarterback of the football team, one of the most popular boys in school. Everything was good for awhile, until she began to witness his temper, that would flare out of control. He was extremely jealous and controlling. Veronica remembered the night he'd had too much to drink and almost forced himself on her. They had only been dating for a few weeks and Veronica wanted to wait for the right time to have sex. He got upset and stormed out of the house, and made the mistake of getting behind the wheel of his car. She found out the next morning he struck a lamppost and totaled his car. He was lucky to be alive. He had been attending counseling and anger management classes. By the time he was done, Veronica was preparing to leave Washington. *Coming here was actually a blessing.* She buried the photo at the bottom of the box just as her phone rang. Her very first call since she arrived in L.A. "Hello?"

"Hi Veronica, it's Aja. How's the unpacking coming?"

"Fine, I'm almost done!" Veronica replied, surveying her room. Her queen-sized bed was in the center against the wall. On the side wall was her entertainment center/bookcase, with a CD player and stereo. Next to her walk-in closet, was her desk and computer. On the opposite side of the bathroom door, was her big screen TV which she placed on the wall. All her clothes were neatly arranged and hung up in her spacious closet. Veronica was now standing at her French doors admiring the view. She realized, from her room, she could actually see part of the ocean.

"So, can you meet Brittany and I at her house in about half an hour? We need to get started on plans for the Benefit Carnival. Oh, and there's great news, Brittany's Dad called the mayor and he said the benefit is an excellent idea and we got approval to have it on the beach!"

"That's perfect! My Dad says he can arrange a news story on the event, so we're sure to have a huge turn-out."

"I am SO excited!" Aja exclaimed. Brittany said that Jeanette is planning a light lunch for us. We're going to be by the pool to work on our tans for tonight so bring your bathing suit."

Now is my chance to meet Brittany's maid, Jeanette. Veronica thought, her mind already forming ideas on how she would bring up the robbery. *Brittany mentioned the maid's name as someone who had access to the house, how easy it would be for her to set-up a robbery. Maybe have a few friends help her out. I mean, she definitely knew Brittany and her Mom would be out of town.*

"Is Bryan going to come with you?" Aja asked, hopefully.

"I don't think so, he's busy setting up his aquarium. Aja, you'll have to come over soon and see it. The aquarium takes up most of one wall of his room. It's a salt water aquarium so he has to make sure everything's right, transfer the fish, it's a big project. He has some really beautiful fish, the colors are gorgeous on them. My favorites are a cute little starfish and a seahorse he has.

"Bryan was telling me a little about it," Aja replied. "He wants to go diving! Do you want to go?"

Veronica thought for a moment. "That would be an experience! The only thing is I'd be afraid we'd come face to face with a shark!"

"Me too," Aja giggled, closing the magazine she had been glancing at while chatting with her new friend. "I can't wait for our triple date tonight. I can get us a discount on dinner. And believe me, it will come in handy, we are expensive!"

"That's so cool your family owns a restaurant!" Veronica exclaimed, as she checked her hair in her compact. "What are you going to wear tonight?"

"I'm thinking of wearing this red and black ensemble I have. Do you think Bryan would like that?"

"Red will definitely match your hair beautifully, Aja. I had a feeling Bryan would fall for you. He's always liked girls with red hair."

"I don't think he's likes me," Aja stated. "He probably just feels bad cause I gave everyone that sob story yesterday."

"Well, we'll see." Veronica replied as her cat, Woody, leaped up on the bed, and pawed at her for attention. She petted him lovingly, thankful her room was now upstairs so he couldn't carry in the mouse or bird gifts he had often caught for her.

"And what about you?" Aja questioned. "I've had a crush on

Josh for two years and he barely noticed me. When he saw you, he couldn't keep his eyes off you!"

Veronica felt herself blush. "He was just wondering who I was. He's really sweet, but I'm certainly not ready to get into a relationship right now."

"As you said," Aja remarked. "We'll see. But I'm glad you're not going to rush into anything. It will be cool to have another single friend to kick it with and do girl stuff. Brittany and I used to be like that but ever since she started dating Carlos, he's all she's thought about. I'm so glad you moved here, Veronica."

"Me too," Veronica replied, as she freshened her lip gloss. "Well, I'll see you at Brittany's in a few minutes."

"OK, tell Bryan hello for me."

"I will, bye." Veronica threw her phone in her bag and gave Woody a kiss. "Be good while I'm away and don't go trying to jump in all the boxes. You are going to get hair everywhere!" The cat eyed her slyly as she gave him one of his extra special treats which he chewed up happily. She grabbed her bag and found her bathing suit and headed down the hallway, stopping to see how Bryan was coming along. When she entered his room, she was shocked at how he had transformed it. In his old room, he had posters of rock bands covering every inch of the walls, now his room looked more adult and cozy. Above his king sized bed was a wooden captain's wheel from a ship. The aquarium was completely full of water and it was bubbling and attractive looking.

"So how does it look?" Bryan asked, mopping his damp forehead.

"It looks really good!" Veronica replied admiringly.

"I figured since we're practically living on the ocean, I should go with that theme. I want to get a painting of the ocean to put on the wall above the aquarium. Where are you off to?"

"I'll be back in a few. I'm going to Brittany's to start planning the Benefit Carnival."

"I wanted to help out too," Bryan stated, hoping to get a chance to know Aja more.

"You'll have your chance," assured Veronica as she headed

for the door. "Believe me, we're going to be planning for days!"

"Listen, I was thinking maybe we could find some cool local bands to perform at the benefit."

"Josh and his band could play!" Veronica replied. "Remember we have no budget and I know they would play for nothing for the benefit."

"I'm sure he wouldn't mind contributing to the cause, plus it's great publicity."

"I hope it's all a success and we can help Carlos' Mom and all the other merchants save the Pier. It's so close to our house and I've fallen in love with it already! We haven't even had a chance to visit all the shops there. I bet you could find some cool ocean knick knacks at *Malibu Gifts* for your room."

Bryan nodded. "I can't wait to check out this surfer shop I saw near *Maria's.* They had some hot surf boards and shorts for sale in the windows, and we have to try out that fish and chips place. You know what? I need to get a job ASAP to support my new beach bum habit!"

"You'll need a job to support your eating habit!" Veronica smiled as she sauntered out of the room. She made her way down the stairs and could hear the shouts and splashing of her little brother out in the pool. She walked out the back doors and found Tyler and her Dad playing volleyball in the cool, inviting water.

"Where are you going, pumpkin? Why don't you join us and cool off?" Mr. Chase called punching the volleyball over the net to Tyler.

"I can't, Daddy, remember we have to plan the Benefit."

"Oh, that's right. I forgot, if you're not doing something productive you are bored out of your mind."

"Where's Mom?"

"I think she's in the living room catching up on her soap. She wants to be up to date for her interview tomorrow in case they quiz her."

"Oh, that's right! Tomorrow is the interview."

"You're going to miss out, Ronnie. We're going to the *Santa Monica Pier,*" Tyler stated, punching the ball back over the net.

"We're going on all the rides!"

"I'm going there too," she shot back. "So I'll probably see you there."

"Good luck with planning for the benefit," said Mr. Chase.

Veronica re-entered the house and found her Mom lounging in the Great Room watching her soap."I can't believe she is pulling another one of her schemes!" she sighed, as she saw Veronica enter the room.

"Oh, I've already seen Friday's episode," Veronica commented as she headed for the front door. "They find out the doctor was behind it from the beginning."

"What?!" Mrs. Chase shrieked in astonishment. "You know, if I get that job tomorrow, I'll get to know what's going to happen two months before you do!"

"And you're going to fill me in on all the details! Good luck tomorrow. I know you'll get the job."

"I'll be so hurt if they pick someone else."

"I'm sure Daddy will put in a good word for you! I'll be back in awhile, I'm going to Brittany's."

"Oh, I almost forgot. Someone delivered something for you a few minutes ago. I was about to bring it up to you. It's on the table in the kitchen. Did you meet someone last night?"

"What?" Veronica asked, as she hurried to the kitchen. On the table was a perfect, long stemmed, red rose with a small card attached to it. She tore it open in anticipation. The card read:

Can't wait to see you tonight!
-Josh

"So who is this Josh?" Mrs. Chase questioned, smelling the rose.

"That's what I intend to find out! He may be a player in this mystery."

"You mean you think he was the one who robbed Brittany's house?"

"Well, Brittany seems to think so. But I can't believe it, I mean, he is really nice," she stated, admiring the delicate flower. "I didn't think guys did anything like this anymore. Who dropped this off?"

"It was on our doorstep."

She smelled the fragrant flower again, and contemplated how Josh could have gotten her address and known where she lived.

**** **** ****

Did I mention I lived on the same street as Brittany? Maybe she mentioned it to him. I'm sure she told him. Veronica puzzled it in her mind as she walked the short distance to Brittany's. *I wonder what Brittany has planned to try and nab the burglar tonight. If Josh does turn out to be behind this… I don't know, I'm just really excited about seeing him. Why am I feeling like this already? I barely know him!*

Brittany's house was another magnificent masterpiece on her street of beautiful mansions. Hers was also secluded and not easily seen from the street. The house was white and had many arches and turrets. It appeared to be three stories. The landscaping was lush and green. Colorful flowers lined the walkway to the massive entrance. Veronica rang the bell.

The door opened seconds later, and she was met by an efficient looking, older woman. Her hair was tied up severely in a bun, and she was wearing an apron.

"You must be Veronica!" said the woman, motioning her in. "Brittany has told me a lot about you. I'm Jeanette Cambridge, Miss Brittany and Miss Aja are out by the pool."

Veronica followed the maid up the stairs from the foyer. She was immediately struck by the emptiness of the house. The only thing that was left behind, it appeared, was the heavy furniture and small knick-knacks.

"So, Brittany tells me you moved here from Washington. How do you like it in California so far?"

"Oh, I've fallen in love with it," Veronica replied. "Although it's a little too hot for me." They passed the kitchen and spacious dining room. *At least they left the kitchen table. How generous of them.*

Suddenly, the maid stopped in her tracks, and whirled around to face Veronica. "You can feel it too, can't you?"

"Excuse me?"

"Can you feel that presence?" The maid looked around the room, as if searching for something she had lost. "Ever since the burglary, I keep sensing this presence, like someone is watching." The maid paused, then returned her piercing gaze to Veronica, "and waiting. But, I love a good mystery, and this one will be solved. Do you like books, Miss Veronica?"

Veronica felt an unexpected chill crawl up her spine. "I love books," she replied, suddenly spooked by the eeriness of the maid. "Especially mysteries."

"Really? Well then, I suspect we'll get along just fine."

"About that night Mrs. Cambridge...."

"Oh, please, you can call me Jeanette."

"Jeanette, about that night," Veronica searched for words she could use without appearing accusing. "Were you here that night? The night of the burglary?"

The maid's smile vanished as she seemed to peer right into Veronica's soul. "Unfortunately, I wasn't," she replied, turning and continuing to the sliding glass door. "And even if I was, I'm sure I wouldn't have heard a thing. My cottage is so far back on the property I couldn't hear a scream from the mansion. The maid opened the door as Brittany and Aja greeted their friend. "Lunch is almost ready," Jeanette stated, as she closed the door in Veronica's face.

I guess that means our conversation is over! Veronica thought, turning and joining her friends by the pool.

"Jeanette is a riot, isn't she?" Brittany smiled, rubbing sun tan oil on her smooth legs.

"That's for sure!" Veronica replied, as she pulled up a chair, and dropped her bag on the ground.

"She is entertaining to have around," Brittany continued, throwing her hair over the back of her chair. "Mom is away on business a lot, so it's cool having someone other than my little sister to talk to."

"I didn't know you had a little sister!" said Veronica, taking her bathing suit out of her bag.

"Yeah, she's with my Mom and Josh's Dad right now. They went shopping for some new things for the house. She's ten, and she can be sweet, but also a complete pain sometimes! Didn't you say your little brother is eight?"

"Yes, we'll have to get them together so they can have someone around their own age to play with."

"I wish I had a little brother or sister," Aja mentioned wistfully, taking a sip of her iced tea.

"But you have Nalu, and he is cool," Brittany replied. "I envy both of you for having a mother *and* a father still happily married and under one roof. My Mom and Dad practically despise each other!"

Veronica put on her sunglasses and leaned back in her chair, enjoying the warmth of the blazing sun. "I heard your Dad called the mayor and got approval for the Beach Benefit. Does your Dad live around here?"

Brittany nodded as she tried not to think about how everything changed when her parents divorced a year ago. She knew they were'nt good for each other and constantly arguing. But still, when her parents told her they were ending their marriage, it was the worst night of her life. Brittany and her little sister, Stacy, had no idea how life was going to be going forward. Being apart from their father since he moved, brought them closer, when they went to stay with him on certain weekends. The girls adored him and it was hard for their father to be apart from them. "He has a new house in Westwood not far from here," Brittany replied wondering if Jeanette was on her way with lunch. "He is a board member for the city, so he has a lot of clout and everyone knows him."

Just then, Jeanette returned with a platter of tuna sandwiches, macaroni salad, and fruit. She set it on the poolside table next to them.

"Thanks, Jeanette!" Brittany exclaimed. "You are the best!"

"Enjoy," the maid replied, with enthusiasm as she made her

way back into the house.

"So Mrs. Cambridge lives on the property too?" Veronica inquired, as they moved to the table and re-positioned the umbrella so it shaded the table more.

"Yeah, in the cottage by the gardens. She has her own driveway on the side of the house," said Brittany as she passed out plates and silverware to her friends.

"She has it made if you ask me," Aja commented, as she helped herself to some cantaloupe. She gets to live rent fee in a cute little cottage and lives on a beautiful estate overlooking the ocean, AND gets paid for it!"

Veronica eyed Brittany, a concerned look in her eyes. "That's a lot for someone to take advantage of!"

"What do you mean?" Brittany questioned, taking a sip of iced tea.

"Brittany, I know you said you don't believe Jeanette would do something like this- but she definitely had the opportunity. She could have easily gotten assistance from a friend or relative to clean out your entire home."

Brittany shook her head. "No, it's not possible. Yes, Jeanette is kind of kooky. Yes, she acts mysterious, but it's just a role she's playing. She loves to get a reaction out of people. She really loves all of us, we're like a family to her. I know she wouldn't rip us off. Besides, she really doesn't have any friends."

Veronica didn't say another word about it as they enjoyed the rest of their scrumptious lunch.

At least we'll finally have a TV again," Brittany said, breaking the silence. "My Mom should be back anytime from shopping. She's still devastated though.

A beautiful ruby necklace that was given to her by my Grandmother was one of the pieces of jewelry stolen. She'll probably never get it back. My Mom treasured that necklace. It was one of the few gifts her mother had given to her before she passed. It's so frustrating something so valuable was taken, and it can never be replaced.

"That's terrible!" Veronica exclaimed. "That's why I want to solve this mystery, the more time we lose, the faster that necklace is going to be sold or pawned off."

"Maybe we can check all the pawn shops in the area," Aja offered.

"There's so many in L.A," Brittany reasoned. "It would be virtually impossible to track it down. Anyway, I have a plan tonight. Aja, didn't you say your parents were going on the yacht overnight tonight?"

"Yes."

"Good. Tonight at dinner, you're going to announce that your house is empty and that you forgot to lock the door. Then, we're going to stake it out and see who shows up!"

Aja smiled. "That's perfect!"

Veronica shook her head in agreement, but something told her that trapping this burglar may not be as easy as setting him up.

"Well listen, why don't we take a dip in the pool, then we'll start on planning for the benefit," Brittany suggested as she gathered up the plates and silverware.

"Good idea! I'm burning up!" said Veronica, fanning herself.

"You can change inside, the bathroom is near the foyer to the right," Brittany directed.

Veronica gathered her bathing suit and headed for the sliding doors. "I'll be right back." She made her way through the house and paused in the foyer as she heard Jeanette's voice filtering faintly from somewhere down the hall. She was talking to someone on a phone.

"We totally lucked out getting that necklace!" the maid cackled. "Out of everything we got, that was the biggest win!"

Veronica felt her pulse racing out of control, as the reality of the maid's words sent a shiver, which coursed through her. *Oh my gosh! I was right! Jeanette IS behind this!* Veronica froze in her tracks, unsure of her next move.

4

Surprising Developments

Should I confront her? Maybe she wasn't talking about the same necklace. Veronica's mind was racing with thoughts as she silently made her way towards the bathroom and closed the door behind her. *She said, "Of all the things we got, the necklace was the biggest win!" It sure sounds like Mrs. Cambridge was talking about the burglary to me.* Veronica twisted the doorknob and opened the door slightly, straining to hear the maid. It was clear she was talking to an accomplice.

"I can't wait to see you tonight," the maid cooed to her caller, in a voice, that as of yet, Veronica had never heard her use. "OK, I'll meet you at seven."

Veronica heard the maid hung up the phone and she was now making her way directly down the hall towards her! Veronica closed the door as her heart began beating out of her chest. Had the maid realized she'd been eavesdropping? Veronica listened as the maid made her way to the kitchen. *I've got to tell Brittany what I heard! I can't confront her unless I have some solid evidence. What I heard was pretty incriminating, but I need something more concrete.* She quickly changed into her favorite hot pink bathing suit. *If I can get in to her cottage, maybe I could find a clue, or even some of the stolen goods. I doubt though, that Mrs. Cambridge would try to hide anything on the property for fear of being caught.*

A few minutes later, Veronica re-joined her friends. Jeanette was no where in sight. She decided against mentioning anything to Brittany until she could investigate further.

"We were about to send the rescue dogs after you!" Aja joked as Veronica returned to the table.

"I wasn't gone that long!" Veronica replied, pulling out a notebook and pen from her bag. "OK, so I was thinking we could all make calls to different merchants and ask for donations of supplies we need."

Brittany tied her hair in a bun on her head and fanned her neck with a magazine. "That sounds like a good idea," she said as Veronica's cell rang.

Veronica retrieved the phone from her bag. "Hello?"

Aja took some paper from Veronica's pad for each of them. "I'll take care of getting the prizes and stuffed animals for the carnival booths. We can call the toy shop on the Pier and ask if they would donate."

"What?!" Veronica exclaimed to her caller. "You're kidding me, that's great!"

Brittany and Aja turned to gaze at their friend, wondering what she was so excited about and who she was talking to.

"Daddy, you are the best! OK, I'll talk to you more about this when I get home." Veronica hung up and turned to her friends, who were anxiously awaiting the obviously good news. "Well, my Dad just called saying his station has agreed to do a special news segment on the carnival, and the possible tearing down of the Pier, so we are sure to get some great publicity!"

"That is so cool!" Aja cried excitedly. "Hopefully we'll have a big turn-out!"

Brittany got up and made her way to the pool steps and descended into the cool, sparkling water. "Their news is like one of the top rated stations in L.A, everyone will know about it for sure!"

The girls took a dip in the pool and cooled off, then spent the next several hours planning the event. They each got on their phones and called merchants in the area to ask for donations. For the most part, they were all happy to contribute, especially every single store owner on the Pier. *Debbie's Book Nook,* and *Cat's Fish & Chips,* offered gift cards, and the toy store agreed to provide all the needed stuffed animals for the booths. *A-1 Lumber* promised to provide the wood and paint to construct them. Chad from the *Surf & Skate Shoppe* promised to provide boards and offered to give surfing lessons as one of the auction prizes. The girls decided to also build a stage where they would have a summer Fashion Show. Chad had no problem loaning guys and gals swimwear for the models in the show.

"Do you think we could get Carlos, Nalu, Josh, and Bryan to walk the runway for the fashion show?" Brittany asked, with a sly smile on her face, checking her list to make sure everything was done. "I'm sure all the girls and some guys at the carnival would love that!"

"And it's for a good cause," Veronica continued. "They better say yes!"

"I'm sure I can get my brother to do it," Aja offered.

"Hey, we could be in the fashion show ourselves!" Veronica suggested. "I've always wanted to walk the runway!"

Aja took a sip of her lemonade. "I'm not sure I could get up and do that," she stated, feeling the butterflies already.

Brittany turned to her friend with a surprised look. This was the last straw! She was so tired of Aja putting herself down and discounting her abilities. She could have any guy she wanted if only she had some confidence. She was always unsure of herself and Brittany wished she knew why. Her brother, Nalu, was totally opposite. He was a regular, all-American guy, who knew what he wanted and was confident he could get it. "Aja, one of these days, you are going to have to break out of that shell your in! You complain no guys are interested in you, well maybe it's because your self esteem is a zero! You know, if you dressed in clothes that would show off your body more, and wore a little more make-up, you may actually get a boyfriend."

Aja stared at Brittany with shock for a moment as her angry words sunk in. Her friend never really voiced her opinion like that before. She felt herself getting hot and angry. "Well, I'm sorry I don't have your fashion sense Brittany, but maybe I don't like drawing as much attention to myself as you do!"

Veronica watched the explosion as it unfolded, stuck in the middle, unsure of what to do or say."

"But thanks for telling me how you really feel," Aja continued, getting up from her chair. "Thanks for being such a good friend!" With that, Aja snatched her bag and towel and stormed through the sliding doors into the mansion.

"Aja, wait!" Brittany called, getting up from her chair and almost knocking it over into the pool. She felt suddenly foolish for being so abrupt and talking without thinking of the consequences. Brittany hurried to the sliding doors but Aja was already out the front entrance. She hurried outside as Aja was pulling out of the driveway in her white *Toyota.* "I guess I hurt her feelings," Brittany stated as Veronica joined her outside. "I was just so tired of her always playing Miss Innocent and being so timid. She always thinks she's not good enough or smart enough to get the things she wants. Aja is one of the smartest most beautiful girls at *Malibu High.* She has a 4.0 grade point average, and always says she wants be a cheerleader, but is too scared and shy to try out. That girl needed someone to tell it like it is. That's what friends are for, right?"

Veronica gave her friend a hug as they returned inside. "I'm sure she won't hold it against you," she said, still contemplating whether to confess her suspicions about the maid. "Brittany, I have something to tell you," she announced, deciding she was not going to wait any longer. She checked to make sure they were alone and Mrs. Cambridge wasn't around.

"What is it?" Brittany asked, with a concerned look.

"I think I know who stole your belongings, and your mother's necklace!"

Brittany gazed at her friend in astonishment as a volt of electricity shot up and down her spine.

****   ****   ****

Aja's green eyes were welling up with tears as she careened down the suddenly windy, *Pacific Coast Highway*. What Brittany said hurt her, but she knew, deep down what she said was true. There were so many things she wished she could do, so many things she could've done, but because she was scared, and not confident enough in herself, so she just decided to not even try. Last year, she wanted to take drama class, so she could learn to be less shy, and be more comfortable in front of people, but she chose office assistant instead. Through most of her elementary and junior high years, because her self-esteem was so low, she was overweight, and very unhappy with herself. Determined to make a change, she started school at *Malibu High* and lost all the weight. Now, she looked amazing, but still, no guys seemed interested or asked her out. The more she thought about it, the more she realized storming out of Brittany's was a mistake. Her friend was only trying to help. Suddenly, her mind flashed to the movie *"Grease,"* remembering the part where Sandy realizes she has to change to get the things she wanted, namely her summer love, Danny Zuko. It was then Aja decided she needed to change her attitude. *I am not going to be Miss Sandra Dee any longer! I am SO TIRED of not going for the things I want!* She had only met him yesterday, but realized she really liked Bryan, and vowed this time, she would not miss out on what she wanted.

****   ****   ****

"What do you mean you know who stole everything?" Brittany questioned, as Veronica, once again, seemed to drag out the suspense by withholding news.

Veronica paused, and took a sip of her watered down

lemonade, collecting her thoughts. "I was getting ready to change into my suit when I overheard Mrs. Cambridge talking on a phone, the way it sounded, I had a feeling she was on a cell phone. She was talking, whispering to someone saying, of all the things she had gotten, a certain necklace was the biggest win."

Brittany stared at her friend in shock, not wanting to believe what she said. Jeanette had been with them for less than a year, but already seemed like part of the family. When Brittany had fallen off one of Aja's horses and broken her leg, Jeanette had rushed right over and taken her to the hospital since her Mom was out of town. She was always willing to help Brittany and her sister with anything they needed. Brittany shook her head. "There has to be some sort of logical explanation," she said finally, hoping it was not true. "Jeanette must have been talking about some other necklace she bought."

"Brittany, I know how you must feel about this, but as I said before, we cannot rule anyone out. People will do horrible things sometimes, when a lot of money is involved. I was thinking, if we could somehow get into her cottage, we could look around and see if we could find something incriminating. Maybe we can even find your mother's necklace!"

Brittany thought it over and realized her friend was right. Maybe Jeanette and an accomplice really were behind the robbery. Maybe she had came to work here to find out the layout of the house and what valuables they had so she could rip them off! "Maybe we *should* investigate further. Tonight Jeanette said she has some important errands to take care of and she will be gone for the evening. We can search her cottage after dinner."

Veronica shook her head in agreement. "Hopefully we'll find some answers!"

****   ****   ****

It was nearing 3pm as Veronica headed for home. So many thoughts were circling around her head. *I know Brittany would be upset if Mrs. Cambridge IS behind this, but at least it would clear Josh and maybe she will actually start tolerating him.* It was impossible to get him, the mysterious rose, or the note, out of her mind. She was contemplating what she would wear for their triple date when her phone rang. Veronica retrieved it from her bag as she got out of her car. Bryan's shiny black *Jeep* arrived with the movers who brought the last of their belongings from Washington. Her brother was busy washing it, something he did at least four times a week.

"Hello?" Veronica noticed by caller ID it was Aja.

"Hi Veronica, it's Aja."

"Aja, are you OK?" Veronica asked, as her brother noticed her walking up the driveway, and acted like he was going to squirt her with the hose.

"I'm fine," Aja replied. "At least, I soon will be. Everything Brittany said was true. It was basically a wake-up call for me. I'm so tired of guys looking passed me, or feeling afraid to do things I really want to do. I'm not going to accept or listen to negative thoughts any longer. So, I was wondering if you would help me with something."

"Of course, I will!" Veronica replied, suddenly proud her friend was realizing her true potential."

"I want to do the Fashion Show, and I want to surprise everyone with a new look. Will you help me find something cool to wear?"

Veronica wondered if she was possibly also doing this for Bryan. "Sure I will, but you have to realize, changing your appearance may not change the way you feel about yourself. Confidence comes from within. Aja, I know if you stare at yourself in the mirror long enough, you will see how beautiful you are! Bryan already sees it."

"What?" Aja asked in amazement.

"He really likes you. He thinks you're cool and he likes hanging out with you."

"You know what, Veronica? I have a feeling the Benefit Carnival is going to be a night to remember!"

****   ****   ****

The next few hours flew by and another warm summer night had fallen. Veronica and Bryan were cruising down *PCH* in his *Jeep* convertible heading for Santa Monica. The warm breeze was soothing as it tickled their faces.

"It feels so good to be behind the wheel again!" Bryan smiled, as he pushed the button on the touchscreen of his radio screen to the next song.

Veronica looked stunning in her strapless turquoise dress. Bryan wore a sweater vest behind a black shirt with blue jeans. They had only been in California one day and already sported tans. Veronica felt a twinge of apprehension about the night. She had no idea what to expect. She couldn't understand why her mind kept drifting back to Josh. She had to admit she was falling for him, but was still feeling like she was cheating on her ex, even though they were no longer together. *This only happens in the movies. Maybe it's the way he looks at me, with those eyes, like I'm the only what that matters. Or maybe it's his smile, that somehow makes me feel good every time I see it. Or maybe I am reading more into this than what is really there.* Veronica tried to put it all aside and not think any more about it. If she did, she would surely go insane. She decided instead, to think about her and Brittany's plan to search the maid's cottage after dinner. *We just may be able to solve this mystery tonight!* The thought of recovering Brittany's mothers' necklace and all their belongings made Veronica want to solve the case even more. *Tonight, I'm sure we will get some answers!*

In Santa Monica, Aja, Brittany, and Carlos had just arrived at the restaurant, which rested on a cliff near the famous *Santa Monica Pier.* The Pacific Ocean could still be heard crashing on the sandy beach nearby. All windows of the dimly lit restaurant offered a perfect view of the sea. It was one of the more famous places in the L.A area. A full moon above illuminated the postcard view and the trio stopped to take it all in. Brittany was wearing a beautiful low-cut strapless top and a mini skirt. Her flowing blondish-brown hair was silky and playfully tickled her shoulders.

"You look so gorgeous tonight, baby," whispered Carlos as

he ran his hand up and down her thigh.

"Thanks sweety," she replied, giving him a quick kiss. She realized Aja had been quiet on the ride up and she really wanted to talk to her alone and apologize for her outburst earlier. "Carlos, why don't you give our names at the desk, we'll be right in."

Both girls walked to the edge of the parking lot. The light from the moon cast mysterious shadows on the ocean and illuminated it for miles out.

"Aja, I wanted to apologize for what I said earlier, it was totally uncalled for."

Aja was wearing a simple, but elegant black and red short dress. Her striking auburn hair was tied back, and as usual, she wore minimal make-up. "There's nothing to apologize for," Aja smiled as she spotted Bryan and Veronica pull up. "You actually really helped me."

"How do you mean?"

"I'll have to explain later," Aja promised as she noticed Bryan eyeing her.

"I finally got my baby back!" he said, jumping out of his *Jeep*. "You like?"

"I love *Jeeps!*" Aja replied, admiring the freshly detailed *Jeep*. "You will have to take a ride in it sometime."

"For sure!" Aja agreed as they headed for the front entrance.

"Veronica, I love that dress!" Brittany exclaimed. "It really brings out your eyes!"

"Thanks! You look great too!" Veronica replied. As they entered the restaurant, she scanned the young crowd for Josh.

"My brother's working tonight," Aja said as she spotted Nalu carrying a steaming platter of pasta and chicken to his tables.

"It's cool your Dad let him work at the restaurant!" Brittany stated, as she spotted Carlos in a large booth in the corner, then felt her heart sink noticing Aja's brother waving at them as they entered. Having Nalu and Carlos in the same room made her uncomfortable. She loved Carlos to death, but she was wondering if their relationship was going to survive. He had been so emotionally absent the last two weeks, and she couldn't understand why.

She was now unsure if they were really soul mates, as she once thought. Than there was Nalu. She had known him ever since he and Aja had become best friends in their Freshman year of high school. Nalu had been like the brother she never had. She had always thought he was hot looking, if not gorgeous. He had dark hair that was shaved on the sides, and long and spiky on top. He was infamous for dying his hair the color of his mood. His body was toned and muscular and he was the typical California surfer/skater boy. But it hadn't been until recently, Brittany had been dropping hints she was interested. Brittany's mind flashed back to a party a few weeks ago. Carlos was working late, and she and Nalu had ran into each other at *Paradise Cove.* He had just finished doing some diving, and he looked to die for in his black wet suit. They ended up sitting on the beach talking and laughing about the fun times they had over the past couple of years. *Why had he never even tried to make a move on her? Was it because of Carlos?*

The group made their way to the table and Veronica felt a twinge in her stomach as she spotted Josh walk in. He was wearing a gray and black dress shirt and black slacks. He smiled when she spotted her and she got up to greet him.

"You look beautiful!" he stated in awe.

"Thanks!" she replied. "You look pretty good yourself! Thanks for the rose and the note you sent earlier. It was very sweet."

Just then, Nalu returned to the group with menus and greeted them as Veronica and Josh sat down in the booth. "Wow! Look at you guys!" he commented, "looks like you guys are going to the prom! So what drinks can I start everyone with?"

"You have to get Saturday off," Brittany interjected as Carlos eyed her questioningly. "We're having a Benefit Carnival to save *Malibu Pier* and it's something you cannot miss."

"I heard!" Nalu replied. "Actually I have the night off, so I'll definitely be there. Plus I have an idea for a booth for a great cause."

"And you're also recruited to model swimwear," Aja said with amusement, trying to say it as no big deal.

"Excuse me?" Nalu asked.

"Actually, we need all you guys to work the runway for our sexy swimwear show," Brittany announced. "But don't worry, we'll be up there with you!"

The group laughed and talked about the event while Nalu took their orders. Everyone at the table was laughing and talking about which guy and girl was going to get the most applause on the runway. Aja secretly hoped her new look would cause the most sensation.

Suddenly, Veronica spotted a couple entering the restaurant, and her heart sank. She quickly got Brittany's attention and directed her to the front entrance. Mrs. Cambridge was walking in with a companion! She looked totally different than Brittany had ever seen her. Unlike her stiff uniform she always wore, the maid was dressed in an expensive looking outfit, and was decked out in jewelry. A sparkling diamond necklace and matching bracelet was the first thing which caught her eye. A waiter escorted them to their table and they were heading right for the group! Veronica and Brittany turned to look at each other in astonishment, just as Jeanette spotted them.

"What a surprise!" the maid shrieked, her face seemingly turning bright red as she spotted them. She immediately covered her neck, as if trying to hide the jewels.

"Jeanette, I thought you had some errands to run?" Brittany questioned, trying to decide if she recognized any of the jewelry.

"I got all of them done early," the maid announced, as her companion sat in the booth directly behind them. "You all look very beautiful," she said, trying to regain her composure.

"And so do you, Jeanette!" Brittany stated. "I've never seen you look as radiant. That necklace is truly breathtaking!"

"Thank you! It's an imitation but still sparkly! Well, enjoy your dinner," the maid said as she joined her companion at the next table.

"I think we'd better freshen up!" Brittany announced, as she, Veronica and Aja got up from the booth.

"You girls look fine as you are," Carlos said as he took a sip of his ice water.

"Well, we need to check for ourselves," Brittany said as they headed for the restroom. The girls hurried through the restaurant as many stared.

"Did you recognize any of that jewelry?" Veronica whispered, as they entered the contemporary lavatory.

Brittany shook her head. "No, but Mom had so much jewelry, I wouldn't even recognize it if I saw it."

"What's going on?" Aja questioned.

"We'll have to fill you in later," Brittany stated. "But we need you to make that announcement, remember? You're parents are out of town and you may have forgotten to lock the back door."

"Then, you and Bryan will stake out your place," Veronica continued, "Brittany and I are going to check out the maid's cottage."

"You think the maid did it?!" Aja asked in shock. "I can't believe it!"

"At this point, she's our only suspect," Veronica confirmed. "Come on, we had better get back out there and put our plan into action!"

Nalu was unloading a tray of heaping Hawaiian dishes onto their table as the girls returned. Everything looked absolutely delicious.

Josh smiled at Veronica. "Is everything all right?" he whispered, noticing a look of apprehension on her face.

Veronica nodded as she started on her plate of Maui beef fajitas.

Just then, Josh's friend, Jimmy strolled in. "I see I'm just in time for dinner," he exclaimed and squeezed into the circular table.

"What up, Jimmy," Josh called giving him a fist bump, and giving his friend a portion of his Lomi Lomi Salmon on a separate plate.

They were all talking and laughing and Veronica glanced at Aja to see if she was going to make her announcement as planned.

Aja caught the look and said suddenly, "Oh my gosh," causing everyone to turn to her with alarm.

"What's wrong?" Nalu asked his sister as he passed out the last plate of salmon to Carlos.

"I think I forgot to lock the back sliding glass door when I left!" she stated, holding a hand to her mouth. Mom and Dad are going to kill me if they find out. Nalu you better not say a word to them!"

"Aja, that's not a very smart thing to do considering what happened to Brittany," said her brother.

"I know," she admitted, eyeing Veronica for her reaction.

"I'm sure what happened at my house was just a one time occurrence," Brittany stated. "There's been no other reports of any break-ins. I'm sure it will be OK, Aja."

"I hope so."

They all dived into their scrumptious dinner as the girls secretly eyed each other as if waiting for something to happen. Brittany turned to gaze at Josh, studying him, while Veronica could see Mrs. Cambridge chatting with her friend at the next table.

How convenient! The thief thought, taking in the entire conversation. *You are a foolish girl, Aja! By now you should know when you leave your house, you should check all the doors. Your place is one of the biggest in Malibu, I just know it's filled with lots of antiques, artwork, and electronic equipment! I guess I just found the next house on my little mansion tour to visit. After tonight is through, I'll be one step closer to getting everything I deserve!*

6

Paradise Cove

I bet Carlos is going to meet some girl at Paradise Cove! Brittany thought as she slowed her car to a crawl just outside the *Malibu Pier* parking lot. *He was probably with her last night too!* She couldn't believe all this was actually happening. Wasting no time, she maneuvered her car into the lot and parked inconspicuously behind a huge truck, near some underbrush. It was another balmy, June morning, and *Malibu Pier* was already packed. *This time I'm going to find out what Carlos is really up to!* She watched him pull in, to the other side of the lot, where most people park if they are just going to the beach and not the Pier. She had called Carlos when she got up that morning, to see if he wanted to go get some breakfast before they met up on the beach to start construction on the booths. He said he couldn't because he had to help with the breakfast rush at the Cafe. The way he said it, made her believe he was lying. On a hunch, she called the Cafe and Maria told her he wasn't working today, and, wasn't she supposed to be meeting him for a picnic lunch at *Paradise Cove? I had a feeling all along that he was seeing someone else! Now he tells his Mom that he's meeting me for lunch when he's really meeting his new girlfriend!* After the call with Maria, Brittany rushed out of the house without even getting ready, to drive by his house, in hopes he was still there so she could follow him and see where he was really going. Luckily, he was just leaving and she had tailed him, trying her best to not be noticed, all the way to *Malibu Pier! I can't believe I'm doing this!* Brittany thought, as she watched Carlos get out of his car carrying a large gym bag, and heading towards *Paradise Cove.*

******   ****   ******

"I get to go help build the carny-ville today right, Bryan?" asked Tyler as he came bounding down the stairs. "You said I can help you."

Bryan took another bite of cereal and continued gazing at his surfing magazine. "Yes, you can help us today, but remember, don't get in anyone's way or we'll take you home. We have a lot of work to do in a short amount of time."

Mrs. Chase and Veronica were making their way down the stairs then. "So how does Mom look?" Veronica asked her brother, while her mother posed. She was dressed in a very attractive business pants suit for her interview with *"Days of our Lives."*

Bryan did a double take. "Wow Mom, you went all out! Too bad Dad already left for work!"

Mrs. Chase smiled. "I will just die if I don't get this job!" she said, grabbing a glass from the cupboard and pouring some orange juice. "This is the first interview I've had in five years! I hope I don't blow it!"

"You must have a positive attitude!" Veronica replied, looking fabulous herself in an off the shoulder top and blue jean shorts. Her hair was tied back and came together in a pony tail. "I need to start applying to some places myself!"

"Yes you do," Bryan confirmed, finishing off his cereal. "The way you spend money, you'll be bankrupt before your eighteenth birthday!"

"Veronica, Bryan, make sure you keep an eye on Tyler, you know how he's famous for running off," said their mother as she fixed a plate of French toast and bacon for her youngest. "Tyler, you listen to your brother and sister or you won't be going to the carnival at all, do you understand?"

"I'm going to be the best worker there!" the boy vowed as he started on his French toast.

Mrs. Chase kissed Tyler on his cheek and said goodbye. "Well, off I go, I hope when I come back I'll have good news!

"Good luck, Mom!" Veronica exclaimed as she sat down to join her brothers at the beautiful dark brown dining table.

"Break a leg!" Bryan called as Veronica gave him a dirty look.

All morning, while Veronica was getting ready, all she could think about was the events of the previous few days. She thought about all the possible suspects in her mind, and was determined to solve this case for her friend. *Maybe the burglary was committed by someone who doesn't even know Brittany at all. Maybe it was just an unlucky coincidence that hers was the house targeted.* She was hoping Bryan had some details he could give about the burglar from the previous night. She didn't want Tyler to know what had happened, and how her brother had gotten into a fight, so she had to be careful what she said. "Did you get a look at that guy last night at all, Bryan?"

"What guy?" Tyler asked in between spoonfuls of cereal.

"I couldn't see a thing, it was so dark, and everything happened so fast. He did seem kind of familiar," Bryan replied, looking up from his magazine to gaze at his sister.

"What happened so fast?" Tyler questioned, upset that he, once again, was being left out of the conversation.

"Familiar? How so?" Veronica questioned, ignoring her breakfast.

Bryan was silent for a minute as he tried to remember more

about the suspect. "I don't know, he just seemed kind of familiar. I can't believe he got away."

They were silent for a few minutes while they finished eating their breakfast. *Sooner or later, we'll get a break in this case, I'm sure of it! It HAS to be someone who was in the restaurant last night who overheard Aja say she left her house unlocked. That definitely WAS NOT a coincidence.* Veronica thought about all the people at their table and the surrounding tables. *What if Brittany's suspicions are true? What if it IS Josh? It does seem kind of odd that the burglary happened not long after Josh's Dad started dating her Mom. What if both Josh AND his Dad are involved?* As much as Veronica didn't want to believe it, she couldn't just rule him out. *I need to talk to him some more, find out more about him. Maybe none of us know him at all, he could very well be behind this whole operation!*

******   ****   ******

Brittany quickly made her way towards *Paradise Cove.* Carlos had disappeared behind the mountain and she was sure just around the corner he was kissing all over his new girlfriend during their secret rendezvous. The fog was slowing lifting and the clouds that often came in to Malibu each morning, were disappearing, revealing a beautiful clear blue sky. Brittany stopped near the jagged mountainous rocks and peered around the corner. Her pulses were racing, unsure of what she was about to see. She scanned the beach and *Paradise Cove*, but Carlos was no where in sight. *Unless he went really deep into Paradise Cove.* Brittany considered finding the trail which lead to the famous lagoon that everyone talked about but few ever found. *They must be back there!* Brittany checked her watch. It was nearing 11am and she still hadn't even showered or was even presentable to meet up with friends. *I'll have to follow him later*, she decided. *I don't have enough time now, but I will find out what he's up to!* She made her way back up the beach towards her car.

The figure watched Brittany run back to her vehicle from the look-out spot, hidden high above *Paradise Cove. Looks like you are getting too close and a little too nosy!* he thought, turning to make his way back down the rocks to the trail which wound along the jagged mountain. *No one is going to discover our hidden treasure trove, least of all Brittany! We've outsmarted the police and everyone else and made thousands! NOTHING is going to stop us now! If I have to, I'll get rid of anyone who gets in our way!*

**** **** ****

An hour later, Brittany and her little sister Stacy, made their way back down the steps onto the crowded beach which was bustling with activity as her friends and other volunteers were hammering, sawing wood, and putting together booths and constructing the Main Stage for the Benefit. Stacy was excited about meeting Veronica's brother, Tyler, whom she had been told all about. Brittany spotted Carlos and Jimmy who seemed to be having an argument near one of the already finished booths.

"Brittany, we were wondering when you were going to show up!" Nalu smiled, wiping sweat off his damp forehead.

Brittany turned and felt her heart leap as she noticed him. He looked good as always in a tight muscle shirt and camouflage cargo shorts, hammer, and work belt around his waist. "Hi everyone, this is my little sister, Stacy."

Veronica and Aja, who had been painting one of the booths, hurried to greet their friend. "Hi Stacy!" smiled Veronica, bending down. "I've heard a lot about you! Wow, she does look a lot like you Brittany," she said, noticing her friend looked a little unhappy. We've been trying to call you. Is everything all right?"

Brittany nodded, forcing a smile. "Sorry I'm late, I completely overslept!"

"It's OK," Veronica replied. "We've got A LOT done already! Tyler, your friend is here," she called to her little brother who was helping Bryan by holding a can of nails.

Tyler nearly dropped the nails as he bounded over to meet his so-called "new friend."

"Tyler, this is my sister, Stacy," Brittany said, as she ran a hand through Stacy's long blond hair. "She's been dying to meet you!"

"HI!" Stacy said holding out her hand. "Do you like to build sand castles?"

Tyler shook his head shyly. "Sure!" he replied, eyeing her suspiciously. "Bet I can build a better one than you!"

"Tyler, you and Stacy can go play by the water, but stay right there where I can see you," Veronica stated, scanning the beach for Josh, who still had not shown up.

Carlos made his way over to them after spotting Brittany. "Hey, I missed you," he said, kissing her on the cheek. "We almost got everything done without you! How does it look so far?"

Brittany looked around, amazed they had gotten so much done so fast. Several booths had already been finished and part of the Main Stage, which was complete with rods to hang a curtain, and included a backstage area. "Where in the world did all these people come from?" she asked, surprised at the turn-out.

"Most are regulars at the Cafe," Carlos replied, as he grabbed a cup to pour some *Gatorade* from the large cooler.

"OK, what's all this standing around?" Bryan called, as he made his way over to the group. "We'll never get done at this rate. I want to finish by 4pm so Nalu can give us a scuba lesson. You're going to go, right Ronnie?"

"I'll try," Veronica replied, spotting Josh make his way down the steps to the beach. "As long as we don't go too far out, I do not want to run into sharks!"

Nalu laughed. "You don't have to worry. You have to be certified to attempt to go way out or deep. I'm just going to show you the basics, we're going to attempt to find the mysterious entrance to the underground *Paradise Cove!*"

Carlos raised an eyebrow. "The underground *Paradise Cove?* What do you mean?"

"You know, the place everyone's been talking about but no one can seem to really find," Brittany replied. "It's supposed to be a really cool spot! I've been dying to find it! I hope there's enough scuba gear so I can go too!"

"I talked to Chad, the owner of the *Surf & Skate Shoppe* on the Pier," said Nalu, grabbing a cup and filling it. "He's a friend of mine and he's loaning all the scuba gear and equipment we need for the Benefit. He said I could borrow a few early to train people who are going to be manning the scuba lessons booth for the Benefit. So whoever wants to go later, can."

"Dude, trying to find the secret entrance to *Paradise Cove* is a waste of time," Jimmy stated, who had been listening to the whole conversation as he was working on the curtain rods for the Main Stage. "So many people have tried to find it, me included, I think it's just a myth. I mean, if you look at the rocks around the cove, there's no place for some underground lagoon. *Pacific Coast Highway* is practically right above it, everything around that area is solid rock. You know people just like to make up stories."

"I know it's real," Nalu replied. "You know Carol Perry, the cool older hippie chick/ fortune teller who owns *Cat's Fish & Chips* on the Pier? Well, she goes scuba diving all the time, and she told me all about it. I know she wouldn't lie to me. She gave me a map to help me find the entrance. I think I may know exactly where it is!"

"Cool!" Bryan exclaimed. "Then we might just find it today!"

Josh made his way over to the group then, and all eyes turned to him. "Hey everyone, sorry I'm late, I was working on my song for the Benefit."

"I can't wait to see you perform!" Veronica stated, wondering if that's where he really was. She hoped today sometime they could somehow get alone so she could ask him a few questions. She watched him closely, as he greeted Carlos, Jimmy, Nalu, and Bryan. *I'm just a push over for cute guys who know how to dress!* she thought, admiring him for looking good in a simple muscle shirt and long shorts.

"So what do you want me to do?" Brittany asked, ready to go to work and try and get her mind off of Carlos.

"You can help Aja and I plan the type of booths we're going to have," Veronica replied, grabbing her clipboard and pen from her bag.

"Sure, you girls go ahead and kick back while we do all the work!" Nalu smiled as the boys walked away to finish what they had been working on.

"The planning is the most important part," Aja announced as the girls found a shady spot to sit on some picnic tables which were brought in so people could sit and eat a hot dog or hamburger near the Main Stage. "If we don't have cool things for people to do, they will think it's a waste of money, even though it's for a good cause."

The girls spotted a big rig truck pulling in to the Pier parking lot, which read *L.A Amusement Rentals.* "Looks like our rides have finally arrived!" Veronica cried excitedly. Everything had been coming together so well, she was wondering if something bad was going to happen to spoil it all. It seemed that's always what happened. They were lucky enough to get a Ferris wheel, some wild spinning rides, a dunk tank, and several games for their booths, including a water gun game where you shoot in a clowns mouth, and whoever pops the balloon first, wins a prize. The company agreed to loan the equipment at a very discounted rate to help with the Benefit. They also said their own crew would come and set everything up.

"We'd better hurry, so we can tell them where they're going to put everything!" Aja said as Veronica brought out a large blueprint of the carnival lay-out that she and Bryan came up with.

"So here we are here at the Main Stage," Veronica pointed at the design. "Over here will be all the rides and the Ferris wheel. Closest to the ocean is the "Save Our Oceans" booth Nalu and Bryan will be manning."

"I thought I was going to help out there too," Aja interjected, hoping she could be near Bryan.

"We don't have enough volunteers to have three people at a booth," Veronica reasoned, besides you don't want to see Bryan before your big surprise!"

"What surprise?" Brittany asked, suddenly remembering Carlos told her he had a surprise for her. *Maybe I'm just overreacting!* she thought. *He could be just going thru a tough time wondering if his family's Cafe is going to be shut down. Maybe he's not seeing someone else at all.*

Aja blushed. "Let's just say I'm taking your advice, Britt." she said, already feeling butterflies in her stomach as she thought about what she had planned.

"And over here," Veronica continued, "Will be some more booths where you can win prizes, and finally on this side, opposite the Main Stage, will be three food trucks from restaurants on the Pier, one from *Cat's Fish & Chips,* and the other *Tuscany Grill*, which I'm told has some gourmet hamburgers, chicken sandwiches, and hot dogs. Then, more picnic tables will be placed all around the chairs in front of the stage so they can watch the entertainment too. The best part is, I made a few calls and we got some awesome gift certificates from the Pier merchants to auction off. We got over ten certificates, from *Tuscany Grill* and *Maria's*, $500 gift cards for Chad's *Surf & Skate*, and a lot of others!"

"Wow, Veronica!" Brittany stated in amazement, you got it all planned out! Remind me to ask you to be my wedding planner!"

Veronica gazed at her friend in shock. "Wedding? Is there something you didn't tell us?"

Brittany forced a smile and shook her head. "Believe me, that's the farthest thing from my mind right now!"

"Is everything all right between you and Carlos?" Aja questioned, knowing her friend was not her usual happy self today.

"Yeah, we just need to work a few things out. You know us, one minute we're arguing, the next minute we're all over each other!" Brittany turned and watched Carlos and the other boys finish up another booth. *Hopefully we'll get it all settled tonight. I'm just going to ask him what he was doing on the beach this morning, and why he's been acting so strange lately.* Just then, Nalu looked over and caught her eye. He smiled at her as he splashed some cold water on his face.

The construction crew from the *L.A Amusement Rentals* had the Ferris wheel and the rides put together in no time. For the next several hours, the gang worked diligently to get everything done and ready for the following days big Benefit Carnival. The only time they stopped was to break for lunch, when Josh, Nalu, and Bryan returned from *Cat's Fish & Chips* with combo meals for each of them. It was nearing 6pm as the girls were finishing painting the last sign for one of the booths: "RingToss."

"I can't wait to take a swim," Aja announced, feeling hot and sticky from working all day. "It's going to feel so good!"

"Yes!" Veronica replied, deciding they needed something to drink. "I'm going to grab us some sodas," she said, leaving the girls as they closed up the paint cans. She made her way to the Main Stage where the ice chest was when she suddenly stopped in her tracks as she overheard two guys whispering angrily at each other. She acted like she didn't hear them as she opened the chest to grab some sodas. She strained to hear the voices wondering who it was. *It's Carlos and Jimmy! They were arguing earlier. They sure don't get along well considering they are best friends! What could they be arguing about?* Just then, her phone rang from her shorts pocket, causing both boys to stop talking and gaze over at her. She acted like she didn't notice them as she answered it.

"Hello?"

"Veronica I got the job!" Her Mother bellowed through the phone, excitedly. "Can you believe it!? I'll be working on the set of the soap I grew up with!"

"That's great, Mom!" Veronica replied, holding the phone to her cheek as she scrambled back to the girls with the sodas. "Now I can come visit you at work sometime and maybe meet some of the cute guys on the show!"

"I'm sure we can arrange that!" Mrs. Chase replied with a laugh. "How's construction coming? Did Tyler behave himself?"

"He was an angel today, Mom. Are you in your car right now? I was hoping you could pick him up, we're going to learn how to scuba dive in a little while."

"Yeah, I can stop by there. I'm only five minutes away."

"Cool! Tyler just loves Brittany's little sister, Stacy. I'm glad he has a friend to play with just down the street." Veronica handed the sodas to her friends and turned back around while she talked, glancing over towards the stage to see if Carlos and Jimmy were still there. They were no where in sight.

Without warning, an arm came around her neck, causing

her to jump in alarm.

"Veronica? What happened?" her Mom questioned, hearing her daughter yell out.

Veronica whirled around and felt an ice cube fall down her back, and Josh smiling at her. "Oh, it's nothing Mom, listen I'll see you when you get here," she said, saying goodbye. She pulled out her shirt to get the ice cube out. "Josh, I'm going to get you back for that!" she laughed, as he adjusted his baseball cap and rubbed his hands together.

"Are you challenging me?" he asked with a grin.

"Definitely!" she replied, as the others came to join them.

"Well, I guess we should call it a day," Bryan announced, taking off his tool belt.

"I think we're totally ready for tomorrow," Nalu said, surveying their accomplishments. "I'm just worried that some jerks may come and try to ride something or vandalize all our hard work."

Carlos shook his head. "I think it will be fine. The beach is almost deserted already and we'll be here bright and early tomorrow morning. Plus I warned the security guard who patrols the area to keep watch."

"So whose going to learn how to scuba dive?" Nalu asked, ready to cool off.

"I'd better go check on the Cafe, my Mom may need extra help. We've been so short staffed lately. It seems we can't keep employees with the possible tearing down of the Pier," Carlos replied, turning to Brittany.

"What?! You worked all day!" she replied, upset they didn't have a chance to talk. "Can't you just kick it with us tonight? I'm sure your Mom is fine."

"I'll stop by as soon as I make sure everything is all right," he replied, giving her a hug. He seemed to hug her extra tightly, like he knew how she was feeling.

Veronica and Bryan thanked all the volunteers and offered them to meet later at *Tuscany Grill*, who was graciously hosting a free pizza party for the entire construction crew. They all agreed to meet there at eight-thirty.

An hour later, the gang was near *Paradise Cove* after stopping by Chad's *Surf & Skate* to pick up the scuba gear and to change into the wet suits. The heat had disappeared as the usual cool evening breeze picked up. Veronica, Josh, Bryan, Aja, Brittany, and Nalu were the only ones left from the group.

"OK. Everyone ready to see what paradise is like?" Nalu asked, as he brought out his gear and regulator to show everyone how to use it. Josh was also certified to scuba so between the two of them, they could train the others.

"I like these outfits!" Veronica exclaimed, deciding she looked very good in her form fitting wet suit, as did everyone else. "If I like this scuba diving thing, I'm going to have to buy my own!"

"Me too!" Bryan replied, following Nalu's lead and grabbing his gear.

The next half hour was spent going over the proper procedures for scuba diving. Nalu showed each, one by one, the ins and outs, then took them into shallow water to test what they learned. Before long, the group was ready to test the waters and apply the techniques. "Is everyone ready?" Nalu asked as he fit his goggles on his face.

"Ready as we'll ever be!" Aja said, totally happy that the entire time, Bryan was helping her making sure she got everything down. He seemed to take to it like a fish to water. She was having some problems breathing through the regulator correctly.

"OK, everyone lets do this!" Nalu smiled as he sunk below the water. The others followed and soon they were all under water! The sun was setting and it was difficult to see everything clearly. Rays of light illuminated certain areas of the water and they all marveled at its beauty. There were green plants and seaweed all around, and dozens of schools of the most gorgeously colored exotic fish they had ever seen. Rock formations were cluttered with starfish here and there. Veronica smiled at Josh thru her goggles as they swam together and enjoyed the whole different world. Josh couldn't take his eyes off how beautiful Veronica looked. Her hair was flowing in the water and she looked like a mermaid, happily swimming like it was her home. They stopped occasionally, as Nalu and Bryan attempted to find the secret entrance to *Paradise Cove.* They scanned the rocks and looked everywhere for an opening. Before long the group returned to the surface.

"That was awesome!" Brittany exclaimed, holding on to Nalu as they climbed onto a rock. "I can't believe I haven't done this ages ago!"

"I was hoping we were going to find the secret entrance!" Bryan said, adjusting his goggles. "It's everything I knew it would be though, simply amazing!" He held out his hand and helped Aja on to the rock.

The sun was setting and created a breathtaking sunset of red and orange as it danced on the water. The waves were splashing against them onto the rock as they all rested and enjoyed the beautiful view.

"I love it here so much!" Bryan exclaimed taking a deep breath of the sea air.

"I'm going back down," Nalu announced as he pulled out his map Carol Perry had drawn for him. "I'm going to take one last look at another area I think the opening might be."

"I'm going to," Josh said, glancing at Veronica to see if she wanted to go.

"How are you going to see anything down there, before long it's going to be dark!" she said running a hand along her wet hair.

"We'll just be down there for a second," Nalu replied, putting his goggles back on. "I want to check one last spot."

"I think I'm going to sit here and watch the sunset," Aja decided, taking off her gear. She was hoping Bryan would stay with her, but was sure he'd want to go back down too.

"I'll stay with you," Brittany offered, wondering where Carlos was. *He should have been here by now. So much for our little talk!*

"Are you sure you two will be all right here alone?" Bryan asked, as he got back into the water.

"We'll be fine," Aja assured him, as Josh and Nalu sunk back below the surface. Then Bryan jumped in and before long they were alone.

The girls were quiet for the next few minutes as they watched the waves crashing around them. "Aja, has Nalu said anything about me?" Brittany asked, turning to her friend.

"I know he thinks your really cool," Aja replied, feeling a sudden chill course through her. "My Dad has been talking about moving back to his hometown in Hawaii," she whispered turning to stare out at the ocean, which seemed to go on to the edge of the earth.

"What?" Brittany gasped, hoping her friend and Nalu weren't leaving her. "That would be awful! I couldn't imagine you guys not living in your beautiful house and being so close as you always have!"

"I know," Aja replied. "As much as I love Hawaii, I just don't want to move there. We go on vacations there to see our grandparents twice a year already."

They both became silent, lost in their own thoughts, as the sun disappeared below the ocean.

The waters below had become even more dark and eerie, and Bryan pointed to a jagged rock formation that had an opening behind some seaweed, and the boys swam over to it, hoping it was the entrance. Just then, a dark figure came out of nowhere right towards them! Nalu's eyes widened and he thought at first it was a shark. As it got closer, he realized it wasn't a shark, but a person, and in his hand was a knife and he was lunging it at them!

7

The Benefit Carnival

Bryan and Nalu fiercely wrestled with their attacker. Bubbles were blocking most of their vision. As the boys started to gain control, the figure suddenly took off, leaving a storm of bubbles. Bryan and Nalu tried to race after him, but as quickly as he had come the attacker disappeared! Bryan and Nalu stopped in their tracks as the bubbles cleared. They looked at each other wondering where the swimmer had went. The boys hastily made their way to the surface.

"We were just about to come after you!" Brittany smiled as they scrambled onto the rock, completely out of breath.

"Are you guys all right? Your acting as if you came face to face with a shark!" Aja exclaimed, helping her brother onto the rock.

"Worse!" Nalu replied. "Someone just came at us with a knife down there!"

Just then, Josh came to the surface and tore off his mask, out of breath.

"Are you guys all right?" Josh asked, pulling himself onto the rock.

"Where were you?" Veronica questioned, feeling a strange feeling come over her. *It couldn't have been Josh! Why would he come at Bryan and Nalu with a knife?*

"I somehow got lost. It was so dark down there," Josh said, trying to catch his breath. "And I saw that diver come at Bryan and Nalu with a knife. I was trying to sneak behind him so I could attack him but by the time I got around the rock he had already disappeared into some cave or something. I bet he knows the entrance to *Paradise Cove* and that's where he disappeared to!"

Veronica studied him, wondering if he was telling the truth. *But what reason would he have for attacking them, unless he was trying to guard something! Maybe the entrance to Paradise Cove!*

"Someone came at you with a knife?" Brittany questioned in amazement.

Nalu shook his head. "Yes, and as soon as I can, I'm going back down there to check it out! Something strange must be going on down there for someone to do that!"

"I definitely agree," Veronica replied, feeling suddenly sick to her stomach as she began seriously considering Josh a suspect.

Darkness had completely fallen and the ocean waves coupled with what had just happened made everyone feel uneasy.

"We'd better get changed so we can meet all the volunteers at *Tuscany Grill*," Bryan said, standing up on the rock.

"Yeah, it's nearly eight o'clock," Brittany agreed, deciding that since Carlos had not shown up, they *really* needed to talk.

The group hurried back towards the Pier. Veronica desperately wanted to talk to Josh alone and question him. She was rarely wrong about a person's character, and Josh seemed to be the type of guy she had been hoping to meet. After everything she had been through with Erik, she *really* wanted to meet a great guy. *I will find out the truth tonight!* she vowed, as they entered Chad's *Surf & Skate Shoppe* to change.

"Dudes! How was it?" the shop's owner, Chad exclaimed as he finished ringing up a customer. Chad was the typical beach surfer boy, with spiky bleached blonde hair and a great tan. He had accomplished a lot for only being nineteen and owning a successful surfing shop. He was one of the top surfers in California, and he used the money from all his tournaments he won, to open his dream shop on the Pier. He hoped this Benefit would bring the merchants the extra capital needed to save the Pier.

"No, we just had a little excitement," Nalu replied gathering all the equipment and hanging it in the closet to ready it for the morning. The boys told him everything that had happened as Veronica, Brittany, and Aja changed in the two small dressing rooms.

"Veronica, did you get a look at the guy who attacked you?" Aja whispered, as they changed.

"I couldn't see a thing," Veronica said, going over in her mind how exactly she was going to ask Josh if he was behind the burglary and everything that had happened. She knew they were definitely going to have to do some more investigating of the area near *Paradise Cove* where they were. She just wasn't sure if she was good enough at scuba diving to be down there for any long periods. So far though, she had caught on quick. "I can't believe tomorrow is the Benefit!" she exclaimed, trying to clear her mind.

"I know," Brittany agreed as she fixed her hair and lipstick in the mirror. "I know with all the publicity from *KNBC,* we will have a good turn-out."

"Well my Dad promised his field reporter will be broadcasting live from the Carnival all day," Veronica stated, exiting the dressing room. "So I'm sure that will bring a lot of people in throughout the day."

Aja opened the curtain of her dressing room. "I am so nervous, Veronica. I don't know if I can pull this off!"

"What are you up to?" Brittany asked, frustrated that her friend for the first time, was acting like she was more of a friend to

Veronica by letting her in on her little secret.

"It's going to be a surprise for everyone!" Aja smiled. "It's going to be a lot of fun! I thought we could use a little something to spice up the Fashion Show!"

The girls laughed and talked more about the show as they re-joined the boys. "Dressing rooms are free boys," Brittany announced as she smiled at Chad.

"Oh, Chad, I don't think you got to meet Veronica yet, she's Bryan's sister," Aja said, introducing her friend.

"Nice to meet you!" Chad smiled, shaking her hand. "I love your outfit!" he smiled checking her up and down.

"Thanks!" Veronica replied, glancing around his shop. "I love the way you decorated this place! Who did you have help you out?"

"I did it all myself!" Chad announced, as he smiled when he spotted Nalu. He'd had the biggest crush on him since they were in junior high together and all through high school. There were many times Nalu seemed to reciprocate his feelings. He wanted to ask him what he was feeling one day soon. They chatted about the "Save Our Oceans" booth and the scuba classes planned for the following morning. Chad was also going to offer surfing lessons as part of the auction prizes.

Aja went over to look at some bathing suits with Veronica. "Isn't Chad the best for loaning us the equipment and the summer gear for the Fashion Show? Definitely a hottie!"

"Yes!" Veronica agreed. "He's *owns* this place? How old is he?"

"Only nineteen," Aja said, admiring a neon green two piece. "He graduated from Hollywood High last year."

Brittany checked out some shell necklaces in the display case. "We'd better hurry," she said noticing the time. "Before all the pizza is gone!"

****   ****   ****

Ten minutes later they were seated inside the *Tuscany Grill* eating their scrumptious pizza. The owner, Dustin Hilton, and his employees were waiting on them hand and foot for all the hard work they, and the other volunteers did. Bryan, Nalu, and Josh were the center of the attention as they bragged about how they fought off the attacker.

"What attacker?" Carlos asked as he strolled up to them with concern.

The boys explained what had went down as Carlos listened intently. Brittany watched him, wondering where he had been the last few hours.

"That's crazy!" Carlos exclaimed, shaking his head. "Why would anyone do that?" he asked, turning to Brittany. "Too bad you didn't catch him!"

Nalu took a swig of his *Coke* while reaching for another slice of pizza. "We will! I plan to go back down there after the Benefit tomorrow and find out what's really going on!"

"Carlos, can I talk to you for a minute?" Brittany asked, as she got up from the booth, not even hungry for pizza.

Carlos looked at her for a second then got up and followed her out of the restaurant. The warm wind hit them in the face as they exited. They walked over to the edge of the Pier and looked out on the Carnival and all their hard work surrounded in a misty fog. "I missed you," Carlos said as he hugged her close to him.

Brittany pulled away. "I thought you were going to meet us at *Paradise Cove?*" she asked, looking intently in his brown eyes, searching them for answers.

"I'm sorry baby, I got caught up at the Cafe. We've been extra busy lately with all the news reports about the Pier and the Benefit. Sales have actually doubled in the last three days! My Mom just hired this new manager and she is getting on my nerves!"

"It just seems we never have any time anymore," she whispered turning back to look out at what she could see of the ocean. Her mind raced and her heart started suddenly beating faster as she decided to just come out with what she had seen earlier that day. "I asked you if you wanted to meet for breakfast this morning and you ended up at *Paradise Cove.* What were you doing there?"

Carlos face suddenly changed, as he stared at her in shock. "You followed me?!"

**** **** ****

"Do you want to take that walk on the beach we missed the other night?" Josh asked Veronica as he finished the last of his *Mountain Dew.*

Veronica secretly thanked him for giving her the perfect opportunity to ask him a few questions. "Let's go!" she said, as she told the others they would be right back.

They walked down the boardwalk and watched as the shops started turning off their lights and closing for the evening. It was an unusually cold night but Veronica didn't feel it at all. "So what are you going to sing tomorrow?" she asked, as they made their way down the steps to the beach.

"I'm singing a song about dolphins," he replied. "I wanted to tie it in to the Benefit. "I'm glad you told me what song Aja was performing, it helped me choose the perfect song."

"I can't wait!" Veronica whispered, deciding she couldn't wait to ask him what she was thinking. "Josh, you aren't involved in any way on the burglary at Brittany's and with what's been going on lately, are you?"

Josh looked at her for a long moment, then smiled. "I know it seems pretty weird that I disappeared when that guy attacked your brother and Nalu, but I *really* was trying to surprise him and grabbed a hold of him from behind. Look at me," he said, holding out his arms. "Do I look like a criminal?"

Veronica couldn't resist smiling as he was trying to be cute, but it didn't help her feel any less uneasy. *He's acting so casual about this. Isn't this a way someone who is guilty would react? It seems it's always the least person you would suspect. I DO NOT want to get any closer to him in case he IS involved!* "I don't want to believe you may be involved, but it was just strange you disappeared right before that maniac appeared."

Josh eyed her up and down, then put his hands on his hips.

"If you *really* think I'm involved, you must be a little scared to be alone here with me right now, huh?"

Veronica suddenly felt chilled as they both stared into each other's eyes and she began feeling more afraid of him with every passing minute. If he was trying to play a game with her, it wasn't funny. "No," she said finally. "I'm not scared to be with you."

"Good, then lets go back. I'm dying for more pizza!"

Veronica couldn't believe he just turned it around like that. Either he *was* truly not involved, or he was a *really* good actor.

**** **** ****

Carlos felt his temper rise as the realization hit him like a smack in the face. Brittany had been following him! "What do you think you're doing?" he snapped, trying to control himself.

"You've been acting so strange lately," she stammered, wondering if this was really a good idea. "I had to see if you were seeing someone else."

"Someone else?! Haven't I showed you time and time again how much I love you?" he questioned, feeling more betrayed than ever. "I'm sorry, I can't be with someone who doesn't trust me!" He shook his head and started to walk away.

"I guess it is true!" she yelled, feeling her eyes well up with tears. "I just gave you and easy way out so you can go be with your girlfriend!"

Carlos stopped, then turned back to face her. "When you're ready to stop tripping all the time and just be with me, give me a call!" With that, he stormed down the Pier towards the parking lot.

Brittany let the tears fall as she fell on to the bench which overlooked the ocean and put her head in her hands.

**** **** ****

When they re-entered *Tuscany Grill* Veronica noticed a lot of commotion going on, and everyone was whispering with another as the owner Dustin Hilton was talking with Bryan and Nalu.

"What's going on?" Veronica questioned as she and Josh sat back down in the booth.

"Mr. Hilton's home was robbed tonight!" Bryan exclaimed turning to gaze at his sister. "We are really sorry that happened Mr. Hilton. If there's anything we can do-."

Mr. Hilton shook his head sadly. "There's nothing anyone can do. I understand there's some thieves going around Malibu and the police are obviously not doing a very good job tracking them down. It's just so frustrating! Listen, I need to go meet the police at my house and see what's left of my priceless artwork. You guys enjoy the rest your night."

Veronica turned to her friends in shock. "How is this thief breaking into the houses? Do they not all have alarms?"

"Not everyone has alarms," Ronnie," Bryan said as he finished off his fourth slice of pizza. "But whoever this creep is, he certainly knows what he's doing."

Aja shook her head. "I feel so sorry for Mr. Hilton! His wife passed away a few months ago and now this!"

"There has to be some sort of connection with these robberies," Veronica surmised. "First Brittany, then the attempt at your house," she gestured toward Aja and Nalu, "and now Mr. Hilton. I have a suspicion the thief knows all of you for him to pull this off. We just need to think of who might be the common suspects."

Nalu agreed. "That's very logical, especially since we all know the people who have been targeted. Maybe the thief *is* someone we know!"

The group stared at one another, too shocked to think one of their friends could be involved in the burglaries.

The next morning, Veronica and Brian woke bright and early to meet their friends and the other volunteers an hour before the benefit carnival was to begin to prepare for the large crowd. They stopped at *McDonald's* drive through to grab a quick breakfast. "I'm so frustrated!" Veronica exclaimed, taking a sip of her orange juice. "I wonder if we're ever going to get a break in this case! I hope Mr. Hilton is at the Benefit today so I can ask him if the police found any clues which might shed some light on who's behind this."

Brain maneuvered his *Jeep* into *Malibu Pier* parking lot which was already packed. "Well, hopefully we'll find some answers at *Paradise Cove* when we go diving later," he stated finding a parking spot. "I think you're right something strange is going on. Now, what were you saying about the fashion show? Aja is going to lip sync a song and you want me to play a long with it? What are you talking about?"

Veronica smiled as she got out of the *Jeep.* "Just please go along with it, you'll understand once the music starts."

"I'm already not too happy about modeling swimwear, Ronnie. What else do you have me doing?"

"It's going to be great! Don't worry. We have to give the crowd some bang for their buck. Lucky for us we snagged a local band to play, so now we have two cool bands. Josh will be performing a song as well."

They both made their way down to the beach. Most of the volunteers had already arrived and were busy putting out stuffed animals, and all the other prizes at the game booths and finishing up last minute preparations. Veronica spotted Aja helping Nalu at his "Save Our Oceans" booth.

"Hey sleepyheads," Nalu smiled, as he noticed them approach. "We thought you'd never make it!" He finished putting out the last of his brochures he had printed explaining the importance of not littering and destroying the oceans.

"Nice booth!" Brian exclaimed, excited he would also be working there and helping out with a cause which was close to his heart. He checked out the brochures and the colorful banner which was hanging above the booth.

"So is everything ready for your big number?" Veronica winked at Aja as she finished hanging the last of the banners for the booth.

"And what number are we doing exactly?" Bryan questioned, turning to Aja.

"You'll see!" she giggled as she and Veronica started walking over to meet up with Brittany who was getting the admission tickets ready to sell at the ticket booth for those who did not already purchase from one of the Pier merchants.

All morning Brittany had been wondering where Carlos was. She hadn't heard from him since last night after he stormed away on the Pier. She glanced up from what she was doing as she spotted her friend approach.

"Hey, so are you ready for the big day?" Veronica asked giving her friend a hug.

"As ready as we'll ever be," Brittany replied forcing a smile.

"Are you OK?" Aja asked noticing something wrong with her best friend.

Brittany nodded, feeling her eyes well up with tears. Josh lied to me. He said he had to work at the Cafe, but I saw him sneaking around at the beach near *Paradise Cove."*

Veronica froze. "What was he doing there?"

"I couldn't tell. I think he was meeting up with someone there," Brittany replied, wishing she would have followed him more. "But, I don't want to think about it anymore. It's almost 10am and we already have a line waiting to get in. We better get a move on."

Veronica and Aja left their friend and did a quick tour of each booth to see if any of them needed anything. They noticed the owner of *Cat's Fish & Chips,* Carol Perry, directing her crew as they were preparing the food truck for the day. She had also set up a fortune teller tent right next to the truck and they stopped to check it out. A crystal ball and tarot cards were set up on a table covered in a beautiful red tapestry. Carol spotted them and left the truck to greet them. "Hello," she said. "We are not quite open yet."

Veronica smiled and admired the way the shop owner had dressed in a gypsy costume. "Is she just playing a part or is she really a fortune teller?"

"She can really read the cards!" Aja whispered as the colorful woman approached them. "She did a reading for me at her restaurant once, and it was a pretty amazing what she told me."

"Oh, actually I wanted to introduce myself," Veronica said as the woman reached them. "I'm Veronica Chase. I think you know Aja Taylor, we are the ones that came up with the idea for the Benefit."

"Nice to meet you!" Carol replied. "I don't think I ever seen you come into the store,"she said, as she sat down at the table in front of her tarot cards.

Actually my family just moved here from Washington. I have to try some of your fish & chips! Everyone talks about it and the portions!"

"Yes you must! What a great idea you girls came up with. I hope we can raise enough money to save the Pier. My whole life has been spent in that restaurant," the woman continued, turning to gaze up at her place on the Pier. "If I have to close down, I don't know what I'll do. This is such a great location."

Veronica spotted the *KNBC* news van pull up in the parking lot. "Well we have a big auction today thanks to you and all the other merchants who gave us gift cards. I know we will raise a lot of money with that."

"I hope so," the woman replied. "Listen, you must stop by later so I can give you girls a reading."

"That would be great!" Aja agreed. "But only if it's a good reading. We have enough bad news already!"

The girls thanked the woman again and continued checking out the rest of the booths. Aja stopped by her booth which was "Ring the Bottle" where you throw rings at bottles and depending on how many you made, you could win a stuffed animal, while Veronica visited the final booth to make sure they were prepared for the big day. Several families and teens were already lined up outside the ticket booth. Their were five amusement rides all together, including the Ferris wheel. Veronica spotted Josh who was ready for guests at his booth; "Hit a Star," where you throw darts at balloons and if you pop three out of five, you win a framed picture of celebrities, cars, or animals.

"Hey beautiful girl," he grinned at Veronica. "Want to try your luck and win a prize?"

Veronica smiled. "Sure!" Then picked up a dart and acted like she was going to throw it at him.

"Um, you want to aim for the balloons, miss," he said, trying to hide behind the booth beam.

"Oh," Veronica giggled as she threw a dart and popped a balloon on her first try.

"Good aim!" he exclaimed, admiring the way she always looked so gorgeous. He hoped they could get closer. The last few days, she was all he thought about. "Are we still going to check out *Paradise Cove* again tonight?" he asked getting serious.

"Yes, I just hope we get a break. I really want to catch whoever is behind this.

"Hopefully we will," he replied, as a young boy and his mom approached the booth. "Ready to try your luck?" he asked, as his Mom gave Josh the two tickets play.

"I'll talk to you later," Veronica smiled, deciding it was time to hurry and check on the first band to see if they were ready to go on shortly. She was in charge of the Main Stage entertainment and also coordinating breaks every two hours for everyone who was alone in a booth. Already there were a few teens looking for someone at the dunk tank but no one was there. She grabbed her clipboard from backstage to see who they had chosen to run it. Carlos and Jimmy! Both seemed to be a no-show. *Where could they be?* she wondered *Don't tell me they overslept!*

Just then, a reporter with his cameraman from *KNBC* approached her.

"Are you Veronica Chase?" he asked looking as polished and handsome as most of the reporters on TV are.

"Yes?" Veronica replied, greeting the reporter.

"Kevin Jameson, *KNBC* News. I knew it had to be you, the way you look so much like your father. He told me to find you so we could interview you for a news segment.

Veronica felt a little nervous suddenly at the thought of

being on TV.

"Don't worry, this is being taped for our noon news, so if you mess up we can do it again," the reporter smiled as his cameraman set up.

Veronica noticed Carlos and Jimmy arriving at the dunk tank and felt relieved as she shot her segment. She felt she had done a good job and gave a great answer when Kevin Jameson asked what the Benefit was for, and how she and her friends came up with the idea. "I believe people should get involved in causes they feel strongly about," she told reporter as the camera rolled. "I'm really proud of all our volunteers who have given their time and a lot of hard work to help out this cause. Not only are we raising money for *Malibu Pier,* but we are also raising awareness to the fact that our oceans are in trouble. With pollution and over-fishing, these great wonders of nature could be destroyed in the near future. We have a booth set up here where you can learn more about how you can help. We are auctioning off over $5000 in prizes. There's so much going on, I hope everyone has a chance to come down to help save our Pier. We also have some local bands performing, and a swimwear Fashion Show, plus some fun amusement rides. The carnival will be open until 10pm tonight so please join us!"

"I think it's amazing that you and your friends came up with all this," Kevin Jameson continued. He turned back towards the camera. "As she said it's a great day, a lot of exciting things are going on, and there is also plenty of food and free parking. Admission is $20 for kids under 12 and $30 for 12 and over, which gives you unlimited rides all day, 20 game tickets, plus a raffle ticket for the prizes. We will be reporting live from the Benefit all day. Kevin Jameson for *KNBC* News."

Veronica thanked the reporter and returned backstage to check on the first band. She spotted Nalu pacing backstage as he was reading over the speech he had prepared to kick off the entertainment and welcome everyone to the Benefit.

"We already have a good sized crowd," Nalu said as he peered out from behind the curtain. "I think we'll get even more crowds later as it cools down."

"So, are you ready to start the show?" she asked handing him the microphone.

"As ready as I'll ever be!"

People were already gathering in the chairs in front of the stage, many of them fans of the local band opening the show. Families were also eating an early lunch of corn dogs, chili-cheese fries, hamburgers, Chinese food, there was something for everyone. Veronica checked on the DJ who was to play the music during Aja's special performance and she directed him to lower the music to start the show, as he announced, "Ladies and gentlemen, welcome to the *Save Malibu Pier Benefit Carnival!*" The crowd roared and clapped as Veronica watched from the sidelines. "And here's one of the hosts of the event, Nalu Taylor!"

Nalu walked out on stage smiling and waving at the crowd. "Good morning everyone and thanks for coming out today! As many of you have heard over the last couple of weeks, *Malibu Pier* needs to be refurbished to bring it up to code, and that's what this Benefit is all about. With all of your help today, we are hoping to raise the funds needed to save this historical landmark. We will be having an auction later, where we will be auctioning off some great prizes and gift cards. We also have some awesome local bands and a Fashion Show. Most of all, what we are hoping to do today is to increase awareness on what is happening to this beautiful ocean all around us. Our oceans are being littered with hundreds of tons of garbage every hour of every day. We are depleting and destroying vital fisheries at an alarming rate. We're losing species never to see them again. California is blessed with over 1100 miles of sandy and rocky coastline. We all need to work together to keep it the most beautiful coastline in the world. The most important thing we can do is to keep it clean. Every year hundreds of marine animals are tangled, stranded, or killed because careless people are leaving trash, plastics, fishing line, on the beach and city streets. Yes, if it hits the streets it could wind up in the ocean. We need more public awareness and we all need to pitch in, and do our part, and take action by volunteering or supporting causes that help. We can do our own recycling. We need to teach our children to recycle. Above all, we need to care, because if we don't, we will destroy one of the most vital resources we have. I hope you all enjoy your time with family and friends and have a great day!"

The crowd, which became even larger while Nalu gave his speech, broke into a thunderous applause. "And now let me introduce you to a great new and upcoming local band *U4EA!*" The music started as Nalu walked off the stage and the curtains parted on the band. The front rows got up and crowded the stage as they danced to the rock bands wild sound.

Veronica returned backstage to congratulate Nalu."That was terrific! How did you memorize all that so fast?"

"So fast? I rehearsed till like 1am last night." Nalu admitted as Brittany ran up to them.

"I had to let you know that was an awesome speech!" Brittany exclaimed, giving him a hug. "What a great way to open the show!"

From his spot taking tickets and handing out softballs at the dunk tank while Jimmy was being drenched, Carlos watched his girlfriend as she was laughing and hugging all over Nalu, yet again. He felt his temper rise.

For the rest of the day, Veronica went around and gave breaks to the volunteers and monitored the entertainment. Aja was to open the fashion show which was scheduled for 7pm, less than a half hour away. She hurried to Aja's booth with her replacement volunteer, so she could start to get ready for her big number. The turn-out was unbelievable and the live broadcast at noon, 5, and 6pm, helped to get word out about the Benefit.

"I am so nervous!" Aja revealed as they made their way towards the ticket booth to let Brittany know her replacement would be getting there soon so she could get ready.

"You'll do fine," Veronica assured her friend.
The group would finish their eight hour shifts by 5pm, then get ready for the fashion show, and after the show, be free until it was time to clean-up the carnival at the end of the night.

After Nalu's speech, his "Save Our Oceans" booth became one of the most popular. While Bryan gave out brochures and talked to people, Nalu gave snorkeling lessons. Not only did the carnival get a lot of business, but the Pier itself was very busy as guests visited the specialty shops to cool off.

Veronica helped Aja get ready in the little dressing room they had constructed backstage, and then checked on the swimwear loaned by Chad to make sure they were ready for the group to change into. Except for a few volunteers who promised they would come and help out, but were a no-show, everything was coming together perfectly. She hoped it would remain that way.

Brittany showed her relief volunteer how to sell tickets for the booth and how to accept credit cards on the terminal, and to be sure to make regular drops so the register was low on cash. She wondered why Carlos hadn't visited her on his breaks. She made her way to the Main Stage and spotted Carol Perry's fortune tent and decided to see what the cards would reveal. She really needed some reassurance about her and Carlos.

"Hi, Brittany!" Carol called as a young couple left the fortune booth. "Would you like a reading?"

Brittany nodded as she sat down at the fortune teller's table.

"I can't wait to see you guys in the fashion show," the gypsy woman smiled as she shuffled the cards and placed them in a pattern on the red tapestry.

"It should be a riot!" Brittany agreed as she watched the woman interpret the cards. Suddenly, Carol's face turned a ghostly white, as she gazed at the top tarot card and realized what it was signaling. "What do the cards say?" Brittany questioned skeptically.

"Brittany, you are in danger!" She announced, turning to gaze directly at her with a concerned and frightened look. "I'm sorry to say this but I see something terrible happening!"

Brittany felt a chill shoot up her spine even though it was very warm in the tent. "Are you sure? What kind of danger?"

Carol shook her head as she tried to get a clearer vision. "I'm not sure, but you should go home and lock yourself in your house. It's the only way to protect yourself and be safe!"

Brittany looked closer at the cards, then at Carol, unsure of what to say or do. *Is this some kind of joke?* Just then, she noticed the beautiful bracelet the woman was wearing, and realized it looked similar to one her mother used to wear. She gazed at the gypsy fortune teller in shock as a bizarre expression crossed over Carol Perry's face!

8

The Fortune Teller's Prophecy

"Where did you get that bracelet?" Brittany questioned the fortune teller, as she stared at in total shock. It could possibly be just a coincidence that both her mother and Carol Perry had the same taste in jewelry.

"I bought this from a young teen selling it on the beach earlier today," she smiled rubbing it between her fingers. "Isn't it beautiful? When I saw it, I absolutely had to buy it. I'm sure is worth much more than what the boy was selling it for."

Brittany realized the bracelet had to be her mothers and whoever ripped them off, was now selling their possessions on the beach! She felt an eerie sensation wash over her. "What did this boy look like?"

"Why do you ask?"

"That bracelet could very well be part of my mother's jewelry collection stolen from our house a few days ago," Brittany stated. Whoever was selling their stuff, she intended on tracking them down!

"Stolen? I am so sorry to hear about that!" Carol exclaimed sincerely. "I cannot believe that boy was selling stolen goods. I should have realized it, since he was selling things so cheap. I bought this for $50, and I'm sure it's worth a lot more." The fortune teller took off the bracelet and gently handed it to Brittany. "You must take this and give it back to your mother," she demanded, feeling foolish for falling for the ruse. "I've seen the boy who sold me the bracelet in my shop before though, I'm sure of it!"

Brittany accepted the bracelet and held it firmly in her grasp. "Did he tell you his name? What did he look like?"

"He was about your age, had a brownish buzz cut, he looked like he may be getting ready to go into the Army," she said, trying to jog her memory on anything else she could think of about the thief. "Come to think of it, he *has* come in before-- with Carlos, the son of Maria who owns the Mexican cafe on the Pier!"

Brittany felt her heart sink at the gypsy woman's last statement. She was sure though, Carol had to be mistaken. *Why would Carlos be hanging out with a thief? Who could he have been hanging out with?* "He came in with Carlos?" Brittany managed to ask as she mentally pictured all the boys he was friends with.

Carol gazed down at her tarot cards as she turned over and revealed the next card. "Yes! I'm sure of it now, the boy who sold me the bracelet, came into my store before with Carlos Gutierrez."

"Then the realization hit Brittany. The only friend Carlos hangs out with a lot is Jimmy! It has to be him! "What time did you buy the bracelet? Brittany questioned, feeling her pulses racing.

"It was around 9:30 this morning," said the woman, just as a crew member from her food truck came up to them.

"Sorry to interrupt, but we are running out of French fries," the girl said, adjusting her apron. "Do you want me call the store and have someone bring some down?"

"I'll be right there," Carol replied, turning her attention back to Brittany. "Remember what I saw in the cards. Be careful, just be careful!"

Brittany nodded. "I will, and thank you Miss Perry." she stammered, as she turned and noticed both Jimmy and Carlos were relieved of their positions at the dunk tank. She scanned the crowd, feeling a sudden chill wash over her. She had to tell Veronica what she learned!

****   ****   ****

"Aja, oh my gosh, you look great!" Veronica exclaimed as she entered the dressing room. "Bryan's going to have a hard time keeping his eyes off you!"

Aja had totally curled her hair and put on make-up and bright red lipstick. She was going to kick off the fashion show by doing a re-make of *"You're the One that I Want"* from the movie *"Grease"*. She looked like a dark haired Olivia Newton-John, complete with red top and shiny jet black tight satin pants. "It took me forever to get into these!" Aja giggled nervously, as she checked her look in the mirror one last time. "Are you sure Bryan is going to go along with this?"

"I told him to just go with the flow. He's seen the movie enough times to fake it with the words. I'm glad you will be doing lip syncing though. I've heard Bryan sing before, and it would be a huge disaster if he tried!" Veronica was already dressed in her bathing suit for the fashion show. A black and white bikini under a zebra print kimono. "How do I look?"

"Veronica, you look great as always! I saw that bathing suit at Chad's store and I fell in love with it! If you don't buy it after the show, I will!"

"I'd better go check on the boys," Veronica announced, grabbing her clipboard. "I wonder where Brittany is. Her relief should have been there over twenty minutes ago!" Veronica closed the door and hurried to the next small dressing room where Josh, Nalu, and Bryan were getting ready. Bryan's first outfit was similar to John Travolta's black muscle shirt and black tight pants. "You guys almost ready?" she smiled, poking her head in the door.

"Um, Veronica," Bryan began, wondering what in the world he was wearing. "I thought this was supposed to be a swimwear fashion show?"

"It is," Veronica replied, turning to search the hallway for the other missing "models." But remember, you and Aja are doing a special number to kick off the show."

"Just to let you know," Bryan announced, as he slicked his hair back. "I'm doing this against my better judgment and because it's for a great cause."

Josh was admiring Veronica in her bikini as he kicked back in a director's chair nearby. He got up as Veronica walked back into the hall. "You look great!" he said. "But I'm not sure I can be a model and walk down the runway."

"You will be fine," Veronica smiled. "Basically you could do anything and the girls will love you. Where are Brittany, Carlos, and Jimmy? The show is supposed to start in five minutes."

A huge crowd had already gathered to watch the show. Luckily, they had set up an area with a canopy to cover the picnic tables from the blazing sun. Mr and Mrs Chase, and Tyler, as well as Brittany's Mom, and Jeanette, as well as Aja and Nalu's parents, Sophia and Niko, were seated in the front row, excitedly talking about the upcoming show and getting to know one another.

Brittany was making her way towards the Main Stage when she spotted Carlos and Jimmy in a huddle with two other boys she recognized from school. She hid behind the "Ring the Bottle" booth and watched them closely. *What are they up to?* She wondered, as she noticed Carlos checking his *Apple* watch, then all the boys gave each other a fist bump, then headed for the Main Stage. The two boys and Jimmy started walking in the opposite direction towards *Paradise Cove.* She wasn't about to let them get away, as much as she wanted to tell Veronica and Aja what she learned, she didn't want to lose the chance to discover the truth. She watched till they were further ahead on the beach, and then hurried after them.

**** **** ****

"Carlos, there you are!" Veronica exclaimed, ushering him towards the dressing room. "Where are Brittany and Jimmy?"

"Jimmy can't make it," Carlos stated, rubbing the sweat off

his forehead. "I have no idea where Brittany is, I was wondering that myself!"

Veronica felt a little uneasy about her friend's disappearance as she checked her watch and realized it was show time. "Are you ready Bryan?" she asked as he exited the dressing room.

"OK, let me make sure I understand so I don't look like a complete fool out there. As soon as Nalu announces the start of the show, I am supposed to walk out on the stage?"

"Yes, when the music starts, remember you are lip syncing to that *Grease* song and you are the one who sings first!" Veronica said as she showed him to the sidelines of the stage. "As soon as the number is over change into your swimsuit."

"Yes Miss Director," Bryan teased.

Nalu was walking onto the stage as he grabbed the mic from the stand. "Thank you," he began, noticing the crowd was double it had been earlier. "I hope you are all enjoying your day here at the *Save Malibu Pier Beach Benefit.*" The crowd roared their approval. "I have to say the turn-out is incredible and we want to thank each and every one of you, as well as the countless volunteers who helped make this possible. And so, without further ado, this is the official start of our summer swimwear Fashion Show brought to you by Chad's *Surf & Skate Shoppe.* Remember, everything you see here is available in store and on his website."

The crowd clapped again as Bryan walked out on stage and the curtains opened revealing Aja walking out on stage near a Shake Shack similar to the one from the musical. Stage hands were hidden on either side of the shack so they could make it rock back and forth once Aja and Bryan stepped into it.

Bryan couldn't get over the transformation in Aja as she was dressed head to toe like Sandy from *Grease.* "Aja?" he exclaimed, suddenly forgetting the crowd.

"Tell me about it, stud!" Aja lip synced to Olivia's words in the song and the *"You're the One That I Want,"* music began igniting the crowd into a frenzy!

Bryan followed her lead and lip synced John Travolta's part, playing it up perfectly. *"I've got chills, they're multiplyin, and I'm los-*

ing control, cause the power your supplying is electrifying!"

At that point, he fell to his knees as she sauntered over, as well as she could, in her ultra-high heels and kicked him gently back, then turned and headed towards the first step of the Shake, then turned back around to face him. *"You better shape up, cause I need a man, and my heart is set on you. You better shape up, you better understand, to my heart I must be true."*

"Nothing left, nothing left for me to do," Bryan continued, then pulled himself up and followed her into the shack. *"You're the one that I want, you're the one I want, hoo hoo hoo, honey. You're the one that I want, the one I need, oh yes indeed!"*

At the end of the number, the crowd stood to their feet clapping and laughing. The gang had been watching their performance from backstage and they rushed up to them as the curtains closed.

"That was great!" Veronica laughed, hugging Aja.

Bryan smiled as Nalu, Carlos, and Josh kept nudging him, telling him to make a move. He looked over at Aja and realized he was definitely falling for her.

Just then, a dance beat started which marked the official beginning of the fashion part of the show. Veronica was the first to go and walked out on stage as the curtains opened revealing a beautiful backdrop of the setting sun. She did a twirl as she showed off her swimsuit, opening her kimono. The crowd clapped some more as she turned and walked backstage. Josh walked out next, showing off his Hawaiian-style swim trunks. The crowd clapped their approval and he danced a little with the music which made the cheers louder.

Backstage, Aja and Bryan were rushing to change in their small dressing rooms. The moment on stage was more than Aja could have hoped for! She overcame her fear and was able to perform in front of people and she felt her shyness start to disappear.

******   ****   ******

The sun was beginning to set, creating a beautiful, natural back-drop of red, purple, and orange. Brittany made her way as fast as she could in the sand, and stopped at the edge of a rocky mountain, just in time to spot Jimmy and the two boys climb over some rocks and make their way deeper into the cove. *They must have some sort of hide-out back there! Could that be where Carlos was going yesterday?* She didn't want to think he could be involved with the burglary of her home. But he definitely knew what we had and the layout of the house! Brittany made her way as quickly as she could, making sure she kept enough distance so the boys wouldn't realize they were being followed. *Maybe this is why Carlos has been acting so strange lately.* She entered the lagoon of *Paradise Cove* and heard echos of the boys' voices as they were laughing and talking. She noticed Jimmy move a decent sized rock, revealing a small opening to another cave! Her heart was leaping out of her chest as they entered the cave. She watched as Jimmy replaced the cave opening with the large rock. Brittany stopped at the entrance and contemplated her next move. She listened, and realized the boys had gone farther in, down a path between two massive rocks. *The secret entrance to Paradise Cove? I thought it was underwater?* She decided she had to go into the cave to investigate further. It was much too late to turn back now!

********   ********   ********

Bryan and Aja were the last to go out on the runway as the audience clapped and whistled. Veronica noticed Brittany's mother, Margaret, and Mrs. Cambridge looking and whispering to each other, obviously wondering where Brittany was. She had a sneaking suspicion something was definitely wrong. Josh was making his way out of the dressing room with his guitar and he smiled as he spotted her.

"Good luck," she said as Nalu walked back on stage to introduce him.

"And now we have another hot and upcoming performer who you have probably seen play with his band on the Pier or the beach. Tonight though he's doing a special solo song. Let's give a big hand for Josh Townsend!"

Josh waved to the audience as he walked on stage and sat on a stool in front of a microphone. It was growing darker and a spotlight was turned on. Veronica watched from the sidelines, anxious to hear his song. She was dying to know what he was going to perform!

"Thanks so much," he said, adjusting the mic. "When I heard Aja and Bryan were doing a song by Olivia Newton-John, I remembered my Grandma loved her music, and used to play this song to me all the time. I felt in would fit in perfect for today's Benefit. It's called, *The Promise,* and it's about one of our most beloved creatures of the sea, dolphins. As many know, dolphins are being killed daily, senselessly, either for meat or because they get trapped in nets meant for tuna. We must continue to fight to save these loving animals, as well as the whales, and other mammals. You can find out all the ways you can help at our "Save Our Oceans" booth."

The audience grew extremely silent as Josh began playing his guitar, in a slow, enchanting melody.

See them play in the moonlight
Watch them dance in the sun
They're the children of freedom-- everyone
As they care for each other
With no question or cause
They deserve to be treasured as a source of love
In their minds there are answers
And in time we will know
What the truth is about all we don't know
They have no room for hatred
Though they've suffered much pain
From the race we call human-- who are afraid of love
If I can only help to right a wrong
With my dolphin song
Then I'll have done what I set out to do
If I can only make one man aware, one person care

Then I'll have done what I promised you
Let us hope it's not too late
And that we can amend-- all the pain we have suffered on a friend
We were born with our freedom
Oh, we were born with the truth
Then why do we abuse if we could choose to love
To love

Veronica was totally captivated by his beautiful and heart-warming song. The crowd was taken as well, and they all rose to their feet as he finished.

"Thank you very much!" Josh said, as he got up and waved his hand again at the crowd and walked off stage. The thunderous applause continued for several more moments as Veronica went up to congratulate him. She started to give him a hug, but suddenly, they gazed in each other's eyes, and then, they kissed. She didn't pull away this time as a thousand volts of electricity shot up and down her spine. As the applause ended, they pulled apart, and she heard Nalu as he announced it was now time to auction off the gift cards and prizes donated by the *Malibu Pier* merchants. Their lips pulled apart. just as Aja walked in on them, clearly distraught.

"Veronica, Carol Perry is looking for Brittany," she exclaimed, trying to catch her breath. "She wants to talk to both of us. She says Brittany is in danger!"

"What?" Veronica replied, as she awkwardly said goodbye to Josh and followed Aja down the stairs to where the fortune teller was anxiously waiting behind the Main Stage.

Carol Perry looked worried as she searched the crowd for Brittany. "Do you have any idea where Brittany is?"She questioned, as the girls approached her.

Veronica shook her head. "She was supposed to be here for the Fashion Show but pulled a no-show. We are really worried about her! Aja said you think she's in danger?"

"Yes, she came to me earlier for a reading. She noticed I was wearing a bracelet which looked like her mothers. It turns out-- it was! I bought it from a friend of Carlos, the son of the owner of *Maria's,* earlier this morning."

Veronica and Aja turned to one another in shock. "From Carlos' friend?" Veronica questioned, wondering if she meant Josh. "What did he look like?"

"As I told Brittany, short buzzed brown hair, like he was going into the Army."

"Oh my gosh, it sounds like Josh's friend, Jimmy!" Aja exclaimed, turning to her friend in shock.

"What's going on?" Bryan asked, as he and Josh made their way down the Main Stage stairs. He noticed Veronica and Aja did not look happy as they approached.

"Brittany is missing!" Veronica stated, searching around for Carlos. "And we know who may involved in the burglaries."

Bryan's smile faded as he heard the news. "Who?"

"We think it's Jimmy," Veronica replied, turning her attention back to the gypsy woman. "Thank you so much for the information. We're going to search the area for her and Jimmy. It seems Carlos has suddenly disappeared as well!"

Josh put his hands on his hips, alarmed that two of his best friends could be connected with this. "I can't believe it!" he said shaking his head.

Aja ran a hand through her hair. "It looks like we have our work cut out for us!"

"Where should we start looking?" Bryan wondered as they returned backstage. "Maybe we should stop by Jimmy's place."

Aja shook her head. "I don't think he is living anywhere in particular. People say he goes from friend to friend and crashes at their place."

"I think we are going to find all the answers we need at *Paradise Cove*," Veronica said, just as the crowd applauded over the final auction of six months of surfing lessons from pro, Chad. "We found all those DVDs burned in the bonfire, and the other night, Bryan and I saw a moving van near the cove, at the edge of the cliff. That is just one coincidence too many!"

"I want to thank each and every one of you for your support," Nalu told the crowd. "Without you all paying $20-$50 just to get into the Benefit, not to mention the countless volunteers who helped put everything together, we couldn't have made this possible. In estimated tallies, we've raised over $20,000!" The crowd roared and cheered some more. "The city of L.A also gave a very sizable donation, as well as other local businesses. We have just gotten confirmation from the mayor *Malibu Pier* will be saved!" The crowd went crazy again. "Please enjoy the rest of your evening with family and friends and thank you!" Nalu walked off stage to thunderous applause and spotted Aja, Veronica, and Bryan waiting for him in the wings. "Wow, can you believe how much money we raised?"

"We've solved the mystery!" Veronica exclaimed. "We have to hurry, I think Brittany is in trouble! We have to come up with a plan quick!"

"In danger?" Nalu asked as Bryan grabbed Aja's hand and they hurried down the steps, through the crowd towards the "Save Our Oceans" booth.

****　　　****　　　****

It took some effort, but Brittany managed to move the rock covering the cave opening. She found herself in a dark tunnel, which seemed to go on forever. She felt her pulses racing as she felt her way along the side of the cave. Maybe this wasn't such a good idea coming here alone. *I can't believe Jimmy would do this to me! He acted like such a friend!* She noticed dim light ahead and found herself staring down into another beautiful lagoon. Water was dripping and barely moving with the tides. This must be the famous secret spot of *Paradise Cove!* The dim light of the full moon allowed her to proceed further and suddenly she heard faint voices and a light coming from another cave opening. She could tell it was the voices of Jimmy and his two friends.

"So how much did you want for the HD 4K?" one of the boys asked as the smell of marijuana filtered out towards her.

"$100," Jimmy replied with a smile thinking about all the money he had accumulated the last few weeks. Soon he could get an apartment, and no longer have to live in the damp, dark caves.

Brittany froze as she realized the HD they were talking about was probably their big screen TV! She wished she could confront them but she wasn't sure what they would do if they realized they had been caught! It was better to go and get help. She had no idea how she had forgotten her phone in the gypsy woman's tent!

"Do you live here or what, dude?" the other boy asked as he fell on Jimmy's mattress and grabbed a bag of his potato chips he had stashed.

"Yeah," Jimmy replied. "Just until I can save up to get my stylin' pad!"

Brittany turned to head back silently towards the cave entrance when she lost her footing and nearly slipped off the ledge of the cliff, causing pebbles to fall with a plop into the water!

"What was that?" Jimmy questioned, looking at his two friends then towards the cave opening.

Brittany's stomach sank as she realized Jimmy was getting up and coming right for her!

****   ****   ****

Veronica, Josh, Aja, Nalu, and Bryan were already at *Paradise Cove.* They decided the boys would search underwater around where they searched before, while Veronica and Aja would search the cove for any clues they could find.

"Are you sure you two will be OK out here alone?" Bryan questioned as he finished getting on his wet suit.

"We'll be fine," Veronica replied, thankful she remembered to bring the Mac Light in her bag today. "Aja, you search the west side of the cove, and I'll cover the east. We'll call or text, if we find anything."

The boys jumped into the water. "Be careful!" Veronica called as they disappeared beneath the surface.

It was very dark and still warm, and the only sounds were the spectacular, crashing ocean, and the faint noise of what was left of the *Benefit Carnival.* Veronica made her way farther into the lagoon area where she and Josh had been the other night. She was proud the Benefit was a success, and hoped she could solve the mystery and make the whole day perfect. She shined the light all around the jagged rocks, hoping this wasn't just a waste of time. She had a sneaking suspicion though, Carlos was also involved somehow, after Brittany mentioned she saw him around here acting suspiciously. Veronica stopped as something caught her eye from the rocks. She shined the light and noticed what appeared to be an opening to a cave! There seemed to be a lot of footprints in the sand all around the area. Her heartbeat picked up speed as she got closer and noticed a path leading between two massive rocks leading deeper into the cave. *Jackpot!* She thought, making her way between the rocks onto the path.

****   ****   ****

Brittany was frozen against the rock wall after reclaiming her balance. She was sure any minute they were going to catch her!

"I know I heard something," Jimmy whispered as he headed right for her. Outside the cave, it was nearly pitch black and Brittany held her breath, relieved as he turned back around and returned to showing off the electrical equipment and other merchandise for sale. I've got to get out of here and call the cops before they leave here! She slowly turned around as silently as she could and made her way along the trail of the lagoon, back towards the opening of Jimmy's hidden hide-out.

Suddenly, Brittany spotted a dark figure making their way towards her and she prayed it was Veronica and her friends! As the figure got closer she realized it was her boyfriend, Carlos!

"Funny how I've been looking for you all night and here you are!" Carlos said with his hands on his hips.

"I could say the same thing about you," Brittany whispered, not knowing if he was there to help her, or if he was actually part of Jimmy's gang.

9
The
Rescue

"Carlos! Thank God you're here!" Brittany exclaimed, out of breath. "You've got to help me. I found out Jimmy stole everything and he's in there selling on our stuff!" She watched him, realizing he wasn't surprised, and then it dawned on her, *Carlos was in on it too! But he can't be! He wouldn't break into my house and steal everything!* Brittany stared at him intently, waiting for his response. When it didn't come right away, she knew it was true. Her boyfriend had orchestrated the whole operation!

"Brittany," he finally whispered, grabbing a hold of her. "I'm so sorry about everything! I didn't want you to find out this way."

Tears were welling up in her eyes and she felt a sick feeling in the pit of her stomach. "Carlos, please tell me it's not true. Tell me you're not involved in all this."

Carlos was silent for a few seconds as he gazed over her shoulder, checking to see if they had been noticed. "I had to do something to help save our cafe," he admitted, realizing he made a huge error in judgment. "I promise you, I wasn't involved in planning any of this, but I did catch Jimmy in the act of ripping off your house, and I didn't tell you or say a word to anyone. He told me he would help my Mom save the cafe. He's totally out of control. He ripped off Mr Hilton, and he's bragged about others he has planned. You know he grew up in foster homes, and has always wanted a place to call home. He believes the only way to get through life and make it, is to steal, so he didn't have to put in the work of a real job. I was on my way to tell him it was all over. I'm turning him and myself in. It's just not right. I couldn't live with myself knowing how much he stole from you and my friends and got away with it."

Brittany felt a tear fall down her cheek as she listened to him. Now she knew why he had been acting so strange, moody and distant lately. He had been dealing with all this! Still, it was difficult to understand why he hadn't turned Jimmy in. He had been over for countless dinners, had gotten to know her mom and sister, had acted like he truly loved her, and now this!

"Please tell me you forgive me," Carlos begged, hoping he hadn't lost her. "You know how much I love you."

Suddenly a menacing voice echoed through the lagoon, causing them both to jump with alarm. "Isn't this romantic?" Jimmy scoffed, as he slowly approached them, with an evil look spread across his face, and a gun in his hand!

****   ****   ****

Veronica made her way through the dark, musty cave with growing apprehension. She had no idea what she was going to find. Just then, she stopped in her tracks as she spotted some light coming from the opening at the end of the cave. She heard some voices and recognized one as Brittany's! She hurried along the sandy cove trail and practically ran smack into Brittany and Carlos! Fear was spread across their faces, and Veronica realized why, as she spotted Jimmy with the gun pointed menacingly at them.

"Well, well, well," Jimmy whispered. "Looks like we now have a party!"

"Jimmy, it's all over," Carlos said, holding onto Brittany. "If you give up now, we may still get a light sentence. Give me the gun before you do something you will regret for the rest of your life!"

"Don't tell me what I'm going to do!" Jimmy snarled, holding the gun firmly, as the two other boys stared in shock from the cave opening. "I'm the one calling the shots here! You should know by now that I intend to get everything I deserve. I've suffered my entire life! First by being deserted by my so-called mother, who was so wasted on drugs she couldn't care for me, then being moved from foster home to foster home, all of them wanting nothing but the extra income. I think it's time I started living!" Jimmy shook his head viciously, trying to erase the memory from his mind. He didn't want to explain himself any longer. "All three of you, move slowly this way and get inside the cave-- now! And I wouldn't make any crazy, heroic moves or you will regret it!"

Veronica felt her knees trembling as Brittany grabbed a hold of her hand, and they, and Carlos, made their way along the trail toward Jimmy.

"Nice and slow," Jimmy warned as he allowed them to pass into the cave. "Sorry it had to go this way. It definitely wasn't how I planned it."

"I guess friendship means nothing to you," Carlos said as they held their hands out and slowly looked around the dimly lit cave.

"Shut up!" Jimmy snapped, as he waved the gun desperately. "Josh was more of a friend to me than you ever were! You were always so obsessed with your bimbo girlfriend to have any time for any of your friends!"

Carlos knew he had to do something fast. There was no telling what Jimmy was capable of! Wasting no time, he lunged for Jimmy. The girls watched in shock as the two boys wrestled for the gun, coming dangerously close to the edge of the cliff! Suddenly a gunshot rang out causing the caves to echo and pebbles to fall, and the girls watched in horror as Carlos face went blank and he fell off the ledge and disappeared beneath the dark water! Brittany screamed as she looked down frantically searching for him. Jimmy turned back to face them with an angry snarl at Brittany and said; "Say goodbye to your baby!"

****   ****   ****

Aja was beginning to get worried as she continuously dialed Veronica's number and she searched the cove feeling an eerie feeling wash over her. "Veronica?" she said to her friend's voicemail. "I'm starting to get worried, give me a call. I'm getting really scared." She made her way back to where the boys had began searching underwater and realized they had not yet returned as well. Aja was surprised Bryan took on to scuba diving so quickly. *I hope nothing's happened to them!* She thought, as she sat on the rock and scanned the dark beach for Veronica, while the salty mist started to materialize again.

****   ****   ****

The boys had swam through the underwater tunnel and returned to the surface once again. Nalu raised his mask, completely out of breath after the seemingly long swim. They appeared to be in a lagoon. "This must be it!" Nalu exclaimed. "The secret lagoon of *Paradise Cove* that you can only get to from underwater!"

Bryan and Josh looked around in awe, amazed they had found the exclusive and secret lagoon! Suddenly, Bryan spotted something big in the water, just popping up from beneath the surface with the tide. "Hey look!" Bryan pointed.

"Its a person, and they are not moving!" Josh exclaimed, as he swam over to him. He grabbed a hold of the man, trying to keep his head above water, and realized it was Carlos!

The three boys were in total shock as they grabbed a hold of their friend and heaved him up onto the rock. Blood was squirting out of his arm, and he was unconscious. "He's been shot!" Nalu stated as he tore off part of his shirt to make a tourniquet to stop the bleeding. He quickly tied it around Carlos' arm while Bryan provided mouth to mouth.

Josh checked his pulse and seconds later, water was dripping and spewing from Carlos' mouth and he stirred, and then slowly opened his eyes. He looked around and then at his arm and remembered everything that happened.

"You're going to be all right," Josh said as he looked around the lagoon nervously. "Can you tell us what happened?"

"It's Jimmy," Carlos slurred. "He has the girls. We have to stop him."

"Bryan, you better swim back to Aja and get help," Nalu ordered, as he took off his fins and stood up on the ledge of the rock.

"All right," he replied, slowly getting back into water so as to not make a splash in case Jimmy was nearby. "Don't worry, bro. I'll get you some help," he said to Carlos and put his face mask back, then went under the water and swam hurriedly towards the secret entrance where Aja was anxiously waiting.

****   ****   ****

"What are you going to do with them?" One of the boys questioned Jimmy, as they saw him come in with a gun pointed at the girls.

"Never mind!" Jimmy snapped, as he motioned them inside the cave and forced them onto the old mattress. "Get out of here," he told his two friends, "and I promise if you say a word to anyone about this- you will regret it!"

The two boys didn't say a word as they held up their hands and made a hasty exit from the cave into the darkness.

"Well I guess it's just us now," Jimmy smiled evilly as Brittany surveyed the small hide-out. She spotted many of their things stacked up in one corner and in boxes. She prayed her mother's cherished necklace wasn't one of the things already sold.

Veronica's mind raced as fast as her heartbeat as she tried to think of a way to get them away from their captor. Jimmy grabbed some old cords he had and quickly tied them up. "What are you going to do with us?" Veronica asked, not sure she wanted to know the answer.

"One thing I've learned," Jimmy whispered to her, "You cannot trust anyone! I can never let you two go cause you would run to the cops. So I guess there's only one thing left I can possibly do."

"Jimmy, Carlos was right," Veronica stammered, suddenly realizing Jimmy was beyond reason and she needed to get him on her side. "If you turn yourself in now, you won't get as much jail time as you would if you were to hurt us. You don't want to spend the rest of your life in jail do you?"

"I've been in jail my whole life!" Jimmy cracked as he finished tying up Brittany. "I have nothing to lose!"

"It was you who tried to run us off the road the other night, wasn't it?" Brittany questioned, praying Carlos wasn't shot and he would come and rescue them.

"That was a blast!" Jimmy smirked, remembering the excitement and the alarmed look on the girls faces as he had passed them in his truck.

"I remember I had seen your white truck at the Pier several times, and the only reason it looked red to us when you were chasing us, was because of the fluorescent street lamps shining on your white truck making it appear red," Veronica realized, as she tried to pry the knot tying her without Jimmy noticing.

"Did Carlos help you rob my house?" Brittany asked him.

Jimmy shook his head. "He found out what I had been doing, or should I say, he caught me in the act at your place when he came there looking for you!"

Brittany was glad to hear what Carlos was telling her was true. She still found it hard though to think he knew who was behind everything but kept it to himself.

"And you ripped off Aja's house?" Veronica continued, realizing he enjoyed talking about all the things he had gotten away with, allowing her a chance to try and loosen the knot more.

"Yeah, I was about to commit the ultimate robbery of all the great artwork when Aja and her little boy-toy showed up! But hey, I know the layout now, so I can always go back! But I got some really good paintings and statues from my old boss, Mr Hilton!"

"You worked at *Tuscany Grill?*" Veronica asked, realizing now, how Jimmy was connected to all the robberies.

Jimmy nodded. "I did, till I quit two weeks ago, just after I was at Mr Hilton's fancy pad for an employee party! All his artwork will look so good in my new house!"

"What new house? Brittany questioned, unsure she wanted to hear the answer.

"There's an old mansion on the street you and Veronica live on. No one is going to buy it after what happened there. I found a way to get inside the house just today, so I plan to move in very soon, he said, excited his plans were finally being realized. Though he never planned on killing anyone, there really was no choice at this point.

Brittany cringed at the thought of what happened to poor Mrs. Winstead, who had lived in the mansion all her life. She was famous for hosting a Pumpkin and Christmas tree farm each year. She was the grandmother of a good friend from school, Charlotte, whose family owned *Debbie's Book Nook* on the *Pier*. On Halloween night last Halloween last year, the family was horrified when Miss Winstead, who was hosting her infamous Halloween party, disappeared during the festivities and was found dead hanging from a rafter in the attic. Since her death, the mansion had remained vacant. She wasn't even sure if Char or her Mom stepped foot in the house since Miss Winstead's death.

Desperate to try anything, Veronica decided to take a different approach. "I understand why you have done all these things, Jimmy," she said, eyeing him closely. "I know you haven't had the easiest paths in life and haven't had maybe the life you wanted."

Jimmy's smile faded as he thought about what she was saying. It was true he had never been happy. It was a relief to think she actually was concerned and seemed to care! All his life he only wanted someone to truly love him. To give him the attention and affection he craved. He despised anyone who was happy, especially the rich, the ones who seemed to have it all. Why did they deserve all the happiness with their fancy cars, huge houses, all the attention and admiration? Why were they always smiling and happy on *Instagram*, flaunting their material possessions, and their fancy meals, at expensive restaurants? It was then, he noticed Veronica for the first time, not as an object but as a person. Could he finally found someone who understood?

"But you can still have it all," Veronica continued, as she finally pried the knot loose, freeing her hands. "It's not too late. All of us deserve a family and a home, someone who loves them. You can have the life you truly want if you work to get it, and realize the world isn't against you. I for one, would love the chance to help make you see the world can be a beautiful place."

Brittany watched her friend, amazed she was making Jimmy see the truth and he was coming around to possibly letting them go.

Jimmy felt a knot in the pit of his stomach and he felt like crying. Why was she saying this? Was this some sort of trick? "No!" He yelled, grabbing firmly on the gun once again. "I can never have the life I deserve. No one cares or gives a damn about me!"

"I do," said a voice from the cave opening, causing the group to turn with a start as they realized it was Josh!

"I've tried to be a friend to you, Jimmy," said Josh silently, inching his way into the cave, relieved to see the girls were OK. "I believed we were friends. We've been through a lot together. I never would have believed you could be capable of doing this."

Jimmy was caught off guard with Josh's surprise, unsure how he discovered his hide-out.

Josh watched him closely, ready to lunge for him if he got out of control, as Nalu waited just outside the cave opening. "Come on, Jimmy, give me the gun. Stop all this before it's too late."

Veronica and Brittany waited breathlessly for what seemed to be an eternity as Jimmy stared blankly at Josh. Without warning, Jimmy grabbed Veronica, forcing her to stand up and he pointed the gun directly at her! She closed her eyes as panic washed over her.

"Now, move away from the entrance and get with your little friend down on the mattress-- now!”

Josh raised his arms as he slowly made his way towards the mattress. “OK Jimmy, calm down. I was only say you can still get out of all this.”

“Shut up!” Jimmy ordered, shaking Veronica and the gun violently. “Just shut up! I’m sick of hearing about this happy little life I can never have!”

Just then, Nalu made a leap from the cave opening and jumped Jimmy from behind, knocking him off balance, and forcing him to lose grip of the gun and Veronica. The boys wrestled and Veronica snatched the gun from the floor, just as Bryan, Aja, and two police officers were rushing into the crowded cave. She helped Brittany out of the cords as the officers grabbed Jimmy and cuffed him.

Brittany was looking around the cave, hoping Carlos was with them, but he was not.

“Carlos is being taken to the hospital now,” Bryan stated. “The paramedics said it was only a flesh wound and he should be fine.”

Brittany let out a sigh of relief as Veronica hugged her. She was glad Carlos was going to pull through!

Josh watched the officers read Jimmy his rights, hopeful he would get the help he deserved wherever he was going. Jimmy just stared straight ahead, with no emotion as they ushered him out of the cave.

****   ****   ****

A half hour later, the girls were sitting at picnic tables of the deserted Benefit Carnival having leftovers from the *Tuscany Grill* food truck and discussing everything with Carol Perry, who was relieved Brittany was OK. The boys said they had a mysterious mission to complete and would meet them at the carnival in a half hour. It was after 12am, the volunteers had gone home after cleaning up. Brittany phoned her Mom, who had been frantic thinking her daughter was missing! Her Mom was happy to hear much of their belongings would be recovered. She had hoped to be able to say they had recovered her Grandmother's necklace, but so far, it had not been found.

Just then, the boys returned from *Paradise Cove* with what looked like a small treasure chest, still wet and dripping. They had apparently gone diving again.

"What is that?" Aja asked, as the girls got up and gathered around them. Nalu slowly opened the chest revealing it was full of sparkling and breathtaking jewelry!

"Hold on a minute, Mom." Brittany cried excitedly, looking through the chest and gasping when she found, near the bottom of the chest, her Mom's stunning ruby necklace! "Oh my gosh, Mom, you're never going to believe what the boys found!"

"Where did you find this?" Veronica questioned amazed at what she saw.

"It was guarding the secret entrance to *Paradise Cove!*" Bryan announced, helping himself to a plate of spaghetti from the *Grill*. "That's why Jimmy came at us under water the other night. He was afraid we were going to find his hidden treasure!"

Brittany began to cry with her Mom on the phone, and Veronica was relieved they were able to recover what was especially important. "Well, I guess this mystery is solved!"

Carol Perry returned to the group with an excited look on her face. "Maria Gutierrez called from the hospital saying Carlos is going to be fine. She's still in shock since he confessed to knowing what Jimmy had been up to, and not saying a thing. She also told me the mayor wanted to personally congratulate everyone who helped put the event together."

"That is so nice," Veronica smiled, feeling totally gratified. "We also found Mr Hilton's paintings and ther boxes of his belongings in the cave." She turned back towards the gypsy fortune teller. "I'm glad we could help save your cafe and the other merchants on the Pier."

"I am so grateful to all of you," Carol Perry replied. "I want to treat you all to dinner at my place when we can all get together."

Veronica turned and noticed Josh sitting alone at one of the picnic tables, surely still reeling his best friend was involved with the *Malibu Beach Mystery.* She sat down next to him at the table. "How are you doing?" She asked, relieved he wasn't involved.

"I'll be OK," he replied, turning towards her. "It's just tough when you realize a friend could do such horrible things. I hope Jimmy can come out of this somehow and realize all the mistakes he's made." He paused. "One thing I do know though," he said with a grin, "I'm sure glad you moved to California, Veronica Chase."

Veronica smiled, realizing she was glad too. This city was exciting, yet mysterious, and different than anything she was used to-- and she loved it. She could not wait for the exciting mysteries and adventures she knew were just around the corner!

ABOUT THE AUTHOR

David D'Antonio lives in Citrus Heights, California with his beloved cat Oreo. Growing up reading mysteries like *Trixie Belden,* and *Nancy Drew,* David was inspired to create his own heroine for mystery and amateur sleuth lovers of today. David is also the author of his memoir, *"Don't Call Me Sir: A Bizarre Journey to Fantasyland and Back,"* in which he gives 10 Decrees for a happy and healthy life.

www.ingramcontent.com/pod-product-compliance
Lightning Source LLC
Chambersburg PA
CBHW051851130726
47987CB00002B/770